A Novel Life

Southern Yellow Pine
Publishing

Thornton Cline

Published by:
Southern Yellow Pine (SYP) Publishing
4351 Natural Bridge Rd.
Tallahassee, FL 32305

www.syppublishing.com

This is a work of fiction. Names, characters, places, and events that occur either are the products of the author's imagination or are used fictitiously. Any resemblance to actual persons, places, or events is purely coincidental.

The contents and opinions expressed in this book do not necessarily reflect the views and opinions of Southern Yellow Pine Publishing, nor does the mention of brands or trade names constitute endorsement.

ISBN-13: 978-1-59616-099-6
ISBN-13: ePub 978-1-59616-106-1

Library of Congress Control Number: 2019953840

Printed in the United States of America
First Edition
May 2020

Praise for the Author

"I've loved reading thrillers ever since I was a kid. From start to finish, Thornton Cline's *A Novel Life* is a captivating story which demands for you to keep turning the pages."

Kent Maxson; Billboard top 10 gold hit songwriter and author.

"*A Novel Life* is a great read. It keeps you on the edge of your seat from beginning to end. In the vein of a Hitchcock novel, a real thriller."

.

Stephen Wrench; President
https://musikandfilm.com
Nominating and Voting Member of the Grammys

Dedication

Thank you to: Terri Gerrell, SYP Publishing, Claire Staley, Roberta Cline, and Lacie Carpenter.

CHAPTER ONE
SOMEONE'S GONNA PAY FOR THIS

Rocky grabbed Griffin's blue oxford shirt, lifted his body off the ground, and slammed his back against the cold, metal lockers in the school hallway.

"See that flagpole out there? I'm gonna hang your sorry ass on it," Rocky said as Griffin's wire-rimmed glasses fell to the floor. Rocky lifted his right foot and stomped them as hard as he could, grinding the glass into the tile. Griffin felt light-headed and dizzy as an excruciating pain ran down his back.

"Aw, where are Griffey's glasses? Boo-hoo, the little sissy needs his mommy," Rocky mocked.

Please, God, not again. I don't think I can take any more of this. That bully has been beating the crap out of me since I came here last year. So, what if I'm different? What if I am the new kid? That doesn't give him the right to make me his punching bag. I'm a seventeen-year-old senior for God's sake. Give me a break.

Rocky Jones had to be the roughest lowlife at William Fentress High. He could have snapped Griffin like a tiny tree branch. Rocky's arms and neck were covered in tattoos of snakes and black spiders. His body was like a six-foot tower with arms of steel. The boy next to him, Bull Dawg Jenkins, was the second meanest.

He was broad-shouldered, muscular, and had a shaved head. He was so tall his head could hit the top of the door frame when he walked into the classroom. His face was decorated in silver piercings, and when he spoke, his lizard tongue revealed the shiny piercings inside his mouth.

"Griffin, Griffin, what kind of sucky name is that, you little turd? You think you're some bad mother, don't you? But you're a loser," Bull Dawg said.

His cruel words made Griffin feel like a fighter who had lost his final round in a crushing defeat while the crowd booed him out of the ring. Griffin wished he had never been born.

Griffin heard the sickest laughter come from both Rocky and Bull Dawg. Big wads of spit flew out of their mouths and landed all over Griffin's face. Some stung his eyes, and some, Griffin accidentally tasted as it ran into his mouth. God, it tasted like fresh diarrhea soaked in piss.

***

That is what I wrote from the memories of Carlton Tucker, the seventeen-year-old, want-to-be novelist. Only Griffin Smith was the name I chose for the protagonist instead of using my real name. I changed all the other names in my book. It was too painful for me to use the real names, including my own. The words flew out of my mind faster than I could get them down onto my laptop. My eyes were glued to the screen, fingers over the keyboard, while I listened to music and locked myself in my room day and night. I had plenty of time to write my novel as my parents had pulled me out of school because of being violently beaten by bullies. My routine consisted of cups of coffee and cans of Monster energy drinks, 24/7. Many times, I'd be in bed by two a.m. and propped up by the computer desk at eight a.m. with my eighth round of coffee. I was on the computer like a determined astronaut spending countless hours trying to get to Mars. Sometimes it seemed like my book was taking forever to write. And at other times, I found myself stepping into the story and living out each scene between the pages. Every word, every sentence, every paragraph, and every chapter drew me in like some gigantic magnet. I was so mesmerized by the words in my manuscript that there were times I felt I had gone back or forward in time with an amazing time machine.

***

This would be the fourth time in a month their fists had punched Griffin's body to shreds like an old discarded duffel bag. The fourth time those bullies had broken out in sick laughter as they chucked massive wads of saliva at Griffin's face. Griffin was too nerdy for them in the way he dressed and acted. He didn't drive a jacked-up ride with spinner chrome rims and carry wads of cash. Word got around school Griffin was a smart kid and wanted to be a *New York Times* bestselling author. Griffin was not the spoiled, rich kid who got everything he wanted. Griffin's parents were common, everyday workers who struggled to pay their bills. All Griffin wanted was to be accepted. He didn't care if he was popular. But there were those in the school who hated Griffin's guts—jealous of him. Those bullies were trying to get rid of him. If they could have, they would have thrown his beaten and bloodied body in the dumpster, hoping he would be thrown out with the trash, never to be found again. They were going to make Griffin's life hell and get him expelled. Unless he acted.

In Griffin's mind, he had transformed into the mighty, invincible, incredible Hulk. He was no longer their whipping boy, Griffin Smith. He had mutated Rocky and Bull Dawg into powerless, indefensible, tiny little Munchkins. Griffin felt a rush of power over them. It gave him the courage to say what was on my mind.

"You're jealous because you've got no talent," Griffin said.

Griffin could see his cutting remarks moved them beyond anger as their mouths curled and their faces reddened. Sometimes Griffin could be an agitator when he crossed those bullies' paths. Griffin had a certain way about himself that got under their skin. It was Griffin's sweet passive-aggressive revenge. Griffin brought trouble on himself.

It wasn't fair those bullies bruised Griffin with their fists, but life wasn't fair. Griffin knew he would have to pay a steep price for his dream of wanting to be a *New York Times* bestselling author. Ever since he was five years old, he had written short stories and dreamt of publishing a novel. Long before he owned a laptop, he scribbled the

3

words that came to him on anything he could find—napkins, receipts, recycled computer paper, lined paper, his mother's blank checks, and even dollar bills. Griffin felt empowered because he had written so many stories. His mother would find his scribblings strewn all over his room and the house, and because she was sentimental, she collected his paper scribblings and proudly filed them away in a hope chest. Everyone said Griffin had promise as a writer. Writing contest trophies and ribbons covered his desk at home. These were strong reminders that he had talent. Griffin had been winning school and community writing competitions since he was seven years old. Griffin was so into writing that he once turned in a chapter of a book he was writing by accident to his English teacher, thinking it was a homework assignment

***

"We're going to bury you," Rocky shouted.

Griffin felt wads of paper being stuffed into his mouth and large pieces of duct tape gluing his lips shut to keep him from screaming. He felt his body raised off the floor by both his arms and legs while he was dragged up the stairs. Those sick thugs treated him like a stuffed dummy they were going to burn. Griffin's whole body screamed with pain. He felt like he was being dragged over a bed of nails. Rocky and Bull Dawg probably thought they wouldn't get caught because of the early morning hour—seven a.m. So much for Griffin's plans of getting to school early to avoid the crowded hallways. Someone must have tipped them off, because this was too well planned. Griffin swore if he survived today's savage attack, he would find those lowlifes and make them pay.

I can't believe my parents sent me to this hellhole of a school.

Griffin heard the bullies open the second-floor, double-steel fire doors, and it appeared they were carrying his body to the bathroom. It felt like every bone in his torso snapped all at once when they dropped him on the floor inside the first toilet stall.

God, what if they rape me this time.

It took every bit of Griffin's willpower to hold back the bone-chilling fear trying to overtake his body. Griffin trembled, holding back the massive nausea bottled up inside his stomach.

Rocky and Bull Dawg chose to beat Griffin instead. They beat both heaven and hell out of him

First it was Rocky's turn. Griffin felt Rocky's shoe kick him in the stomach and face. His fist must have punched every part of Griffin at least twenty times. Griffin desperately gasped for breath as the pain tormented his body.

God, I wish I had never bragged all those times about how I was going to write a New York Times *bestselling novel and how I would become rich and famous.*

Griffin saw his pale skin turn to blue with every fist that landed on his flesh. He smelled blood from the force of the fists. Then Bull Dawg, not to be outdone by Rocky, took his turn. They were cursing and swearing. "Mother this and mother that." They egged each other on.

I only wanted to write a book so someone in this world would notice me. My parents never loved me, never showed me any attention.

Bull Dawg continued with his sadistic tactics. Griffin watched, terrified, as Bull Dawg lifted the toilet seat and proceeded to take a wicked piss in the bowl. Griffin felt Bull Dawg tie a rope around his legs and throw the other end of the rope over a steel three-inch pipe hanging from the ceiling.

"You're going under," Bull Dawg laughed sadistically.

I pray the janitor doesn't find my remains lying on the floor inside the bathroom stall when he's cleaning tonight.

Griffin felt his lungs and voice box working overtime to force a scream through his duct-taped mouth. But it was impossible for anyone to hear him.

If I could write a bestselling novel and I could become famous it would make my parents proud of me. Maybe for once they would notice me.

5

All at once, Griffin swung his fists into the air. He hit Bull Dawg in the nuts as his body was pulled by the rope tied around his feet. Griffin saw stars in his eyes, and he felt nausea well up from inside the pit of his stomach as his body was hung upside down over the toilet bowl.

Griffin was no longer the mighty, incredible, invincible Hulk. And they were not the powerless Munchkins. This time his mind transported him back in time and morphed him into Gulliver. He was in the strange land out of *Gulliver's Travels*, being tied up by the tiny citizens of the island of Lilliput.

"Take this, you little sissy," Rocky said.

***

Sometimes the pain and hurt were so unbearable. Sometimes the story was too close to me to tell. I had to step away from it all for a while. I was still Carlton Tucker, and this really did happen to me. But I could never find a reason to use my real name in my novel. What those bastards did to me was unforgivable. I relived those violent moments in my dreams and in my mind. Sometimes I wanted to kill them in cold blood. I was passive-aggressive through and through.

***

Griffin believed he was going to die. He watched with sheer terror as his head and face were lowered into the two feet of water and piss. God, it tasted foul as it went up his nose, and his stomach rolled. Griffin's eyes burned. Rocky and Bull Dawg pulled him out of the bowl as he desperately gasped and choked for breath. Then, Griffin was in freefall. His body was dropped from the ceiling, and they dragged him to the center of the room. They laughed, unzipping their flies and pissing all over Griffin; the warm urine soaked his body. Before they could finish, Griffin caught a glimpse of Coach Jackson from the corner of his eye, panic-faced, running into the bathroom.

"What the heck is going on?" Coach shouted.

6

Coach was piping mad at the barbaric scene. Griffin watched Coach Jackson rush Rocky and grab his arms from behind, Rocky still in shock. It looked like Bull Dawg was paralyzed, not knowing what to do.

Saved, just in time.

Griffin sighed and relaxed, his mind imagined orchestrating the rescue by the brave Portuguese Captain Pedro de Méndez, who would free him from the tiny little citizens of Lilliput Island and take him to a new land.

Griffin watched Coach Jackson hold Rocky with his arms behind his back so he couldn't move.

***

The moment felt like only yesterday since that awful act of violence happened. It would be the end of my school days spent at William Fentress High.

***

Not a second later, Principal Jones stormed into the bathroom.

"Don't anyone move," he shouted. I watched him yank Bull Dawg by the arms and pull him out into the hallway.

Thank God, I was still alive to witness justice being served.

Griffin's skin felt water-soaked from lying in the pool of urine.

Unbelievable. The author of Gulliver's Travels, *Jonathan Swift, has just rescued me.*

Griffin was on the edge of blacking out when he heard Principal Jones order Bull Dawg to lie face down on the floor while Coach Jackson still held onto Rocky. Then Jones returned to the bathroom.

"Are you okay, Griffin? Can you move?" *Jonathan Swift* asked, but then Griffin looked up and saw Principal Jones.

Griffin felt his lips trying to move to speak, but his mouth was too full of wads of paper, and his lips were still duct-taped shut. His frail body was too weak, his arms and legs trembling, and his feet numb as if the blood didn't flow there anymore.

Someone, please, untie my feet.

Griffin felt Principal Jones slowly pull the tape from his lips and clear his mouth. He felt an intense burning pain on the skin of his face with each jerk of Jones's hand. It sent shivers through his body.

"Ouch, dammit!" I screamed. Principal Jones nearly ripped the skin off my lips.

"Are you hurt?"

Griffin didn't say a word.

He watched as Principal Jones untied Griffin's feet.

When will I feel anything again?

Principal Jones moved Griffin's arms and legs to see if anything was broken.

Thank you for saving my life, Mr. Swift.

Griffin pretended to be okay for fear of ratting out Rocky and Bull Dawg. There would be revenge and repercussions if Griffin told what really happened to him. It took a lot of guts not to say what Griffin wanted to say to the legendary author, *Mr. Jonathan Swift*, aka, Principal Jones.

"I'll be alright," Griffin finally replied, his voice trembling.

Every ounce of his body hurt. Griffin felt as if he could never walk again., He felt like a wounded and defeated soldier returning from war. But Griffin didn't want to admit it.

He watched Principal Jones radio on his walkie-talkie.

"Officer, I need security now for the second-floor boy's bathroom."

Four Chicago Police officers rushed to the scene within minutes.

"We're going to my office, and we'll get to the bottom of this now," Principal Jones ordered.

Griffin gleefully watched the officers grab Rocky and Bull Dawg by the arms and drag them down the hallway to the stairwell. Coach Jackson and Principal Jones wiped the urine and blood off Griffin's skin. Griffin felt the dry, clean towels glide over his skin. They handed him a school T-shirt to wear, and then they escorted him straight to the office.

The office doors slammed behind Mr. Jones as Griffin, Rocky and Bull Dawg stepped inside. Griffin felt outnumbered, surrounded by officers and teachers.

"Sit down and shut up!"

Rocky and Bull Dawg took a seat across from Griffin. No one said a word.

"What just happened back there?" Principal Jones demanded, his voice stern and forceful.

Silence overwhelmed the room. No one dared to speak.

"Okay, fine, if that's the way you want to play this game, then we can sit here all day until you talk to me."

Gee thanks, Mr. Swift. Some author you are. Can't you think of a better line?

"Okay, we're going to hear each one of you tell us exactly what happened in the bathroom."

As the silence continued, no one wanted to rat out the other. Griffin knew Bull Dawg and Rocky would contemplate slitting his throat if he spoke now.

Principal Jones used his best interrogation tactics, but the homies sat there slumped in their chairs, never once opened their mouths, and kept their arms folded for two hours.

"Alright, if no one's going to talk, then you are not welcome back in this school again."

Principal Jones looked straight into Rocky and Bull Dawg's eyes. Silence hung heavily over the room.

"Did you hear what I just said? You two are expelled. I will contact your parents immediately."

Good riddance, you assholes.

The officers grabbed Rocky and Bull Dawg's arms, removed them from their chairs, and escorted them to their cars outside in the school parking lot.

Principal Jones closed his office door and took a seat behind his desk. The silence between Griffin and Principal Jones was deafening. Jones looked Griffin square in the eyes and spoke.

"I sincerely apologize to you for what happened today in the bathroom. You are free to talk now since we have removed those bullies. The police will be filing a report on this senseless attack. Please tell them everything that happened. Don't keep anything from them."

Griffin didn't say a word. He shook his head to acknowledge Principal Jones.

"I will call your parents while you talk to the officers."

CHAPTER TWO
A MAD RETREAT

That dreadful, violent day was still fresh on my mind. It was the day that started my novel writing and ended my days at William Fentress High. It pains me to admit it but if it wasn't for that day, I would have never started writing my novel. It's strange but true. That painful, hurtful moment was a catalyst that began a chain reaction. My parents pulled me out of school; it gave me 24/7 to write my novel, and it gave me this story to write.

***

After Griffin was interviewed by the police, Principal Jones sent him home early. Jones figured Griffin had too much trauma to handle in one day. Griffin managed to limp out of the principal's office, get his stuff from his locker, and hobble out of the school to his 1998 Plymouth Breeze in the parking lot. He was still raging, piping-hot mad over being brutally attacked in the bathroom earlier. He felt the urge to put his fists through a wall or beat the crap out of the first person that stood in his way.

Griffin managed to position himself in the driver's seat even though his body hurt like hell and was bruised all over. He fired up the ignition and gunned his slow, *piece of junk,* car as fast as it would take him out of the parking lot. Griffin watched in his rear-view mirror as he left a trail of burnt rubber on the blacktop. He raced onto Pershing Road and drove like a madman toward I-90. Once Griffin pulled onto I-90, he felt like Superman flying faster than speeding bullets. The only difference was that Griffin was flying almost one hundred miles an hour in his junky old car. Griffin felt as mad as an army of swarming wasps ready to attack. Lucky for him, there were no cops around to pull him over as he drove to the Calumet River.

Griffin felt the warmth of the sunny October day touching his face. At the same time, he felt a dark cloud hanging over him. Something was drastically wrong, but Griffin couldn't put his finger on it. At the moment, Griffin didn't like the person he had become. He felt sorry for himself and was determined to spend the rest of the day throwing himself a pity party. He felt the thick grass cushion his butt as he sat on the banks of the river, trying to figure out just what had happened that morning and why he felt so angry.

A large black and gray cargo ship moved at a tortoise-pace down the river. Griffin could've sworn he saw the captain laughing at him as if he was some dumb-ass clown. The captain was mocking Griffin like he was the biggest fool in all of Chicago.

"You stupid kid, you're never going to amount to anything," Griffin thought he heard the captain say.

Griffin didn't care if his parents were worried or not.

They never worried about me before. why should they care about me now?

Griffin didn't care if he ever made it home.

They probably won't miss me.

His mom and dad wouldn't understand anyway. His dad would tell him to toughen up and not be a sissy. His father never cared much for *weaklings, sissies, or girly boys.*

I'll never live up to his expectations of what a "strong, macho" son should be.

Griffin's mom never quite understood him either. She seemed to be oblivious of his troubles, living in her own world. Perhaps it was a coping mechanism. Maybe she was living a life of denial, because it was too painful to face the reality of being married to a dad like he had. Griffin lamented about his family and school life being messed up

They treat me like some worthless piece of trash.

Griffin sat tensely on the edge of the bank, aimlessly throwing rocks into the river. His anger grew stronger by the second. If anything, or anyone had gotten in his way, Griffin would have tried to beat the crap out of them.

This was supposed to me my senior year. It was supposed to be the best time of my life. They ruined everything.

Griffin felt like a fizzy, liter bottle of soda pop that had been shaken one too many times. He watched large ripples and waves form as he forcefully threw a fist full of gravel into the water. Griffin yelled to the top of his lungs as he let go of himself in a fit of rage. They probably heard Griffin all the way to Navy Pier.

Hours passed as Griffin thought about what to do. He imagined every possible way he could carry out his revenge. Griffin saw himself setting them up for a crime they hadn't committed. He pictured them being hauled off in cuffs to prison while he laughed his ass off. Griffin saw himself dousing Rocky and Bull Dawg's bodies with gasoline while tied up to a tree. He watched himself flick the cig lighter to set them on fire. Griffin imagined their bodies burning to blackened, charred corpses. He watched himself plant a bomb inside each one of their cars, wired to their ignition and starter. Griffin would watch from a distance, as each one blew up into tiny pieces as they turned the keys. Griffin even thought of using what little money he had left in his bank account and hiring a hitman to do these dirty deeds.

Griffin sat in silence. He thought long and hard about his evil, violent thoughts of revenge towards Rocky and Bull Dawg.

What kind of sick person would do those heinous crimes?

Griffin shuddered to think he had become a cold-hearted, hateful and revengeful person. That wasn't the person he wanted to be for the rest of his life.

What good would it do to seek revenge? Rocky and Bull Dawg would only get me back. It would never stop until someone got killed.

***

Griffin continued to search his heart. He dug deeper and searched harder than before. All at once, a wave of compassion overtook

13

Griffin. It was as if he had been released from his revengeful and hateful spirit. He felt something powerful tugging at his heart and soul. Something Griffin couldn't explain. All he knew was he wasn't the same. Suddenly Griffin felt the desire in his heart to become bigger than all the hate and revenge. He wanted to rise above it all. Griffin thought about what he could do to change his life and change his ugly attitude. He also wondered why those bully attacks happened in the first place. Had he done something to provoke Rocky and Bull Dawg? Had he called too much attention to himself by bragging too much?

Griffin decided he'd had enough of his whining and complaining. He could complain his whole life away, but if he never took any action, he would become a slave to his own anger, hurt, fears, and the issues he had with his parents. Enough was enough. Griffin needed to break free of all that pain and anguish. If he had to see a psych doctor or get some therapy, he was willing to do so. He made up his mind to change his attitude and his life. He stood, lifted his hands to the sky, and shouted to the heavens above, "You can't hurt me anymore, Rocky and Bull Dawg. I won't let you."

Griffin took a deep breath and continued to shout, "I'm going to rise above this. I'm going to be bigger and stronger than you."

That was the first step Griffin took toward releasing his pent-up anger and facing the issues that followed him around like a ghost from yesterday. He knew he still had a long way to go. He had to deal with all the issues with his parents and how he was raised. But that would come another day. Today, Griffin had achieved a milestone. He was letting go of his enemies and his hatred for them. Griffin would no longer seek revenge but he'd show his love for them.

CHAPTER THREE
THE DREADED TALK WITH MY PARENTS

"I wonder if my parents would miss me if I walked out into this river right now and ended it all," Griffin said to himself.

Griffin paused for a moment to think about his next plan of action.

I wonder if dying is as nice as people say... the bright light, the warmth. It would be better than having to face my parents, Griffin thought.

He listened, but no one answered

***

These memories all came back to me in a flash. I remember those painful times when nothing seemed to matter, and nothing made sense anymore. This was a defining moment in my life.

***

The sun began to meet the horizon. Griffin spent hours at the river and never told his parents. His phone screen lit up with missed calls and texts from his mom and dad. That surprised him, as Griffin believed they wouldn't miss him. The likely story was they were piping mad and couldn't wait to unleash their wrath on him. Griffin kept avoiding their messages like someone trying to avoid the stomach virus. If only he could muster up the courage of Hercules. His black and white Converse shoes carried his body back and forth along the riverbank as he attempted to calm down. He picked up a few more rocks and hurled them into the river before his faithful

Converses carried him to his car. With a blank stare, Griffin saw his eyes looking back at him in the rear-view mirror. It was crunch time; the moment of truth.

What am I going to tell Mom and Dad?

Disturbing pictures and angry words ran through Griffin's mind.

They're going to be pissed and will want to know where I've been.

Griffin swallowed the little pride he had left, started his car, drove north on South Doty Avenue and merged onto I-94 North toward his house. As he drove, Griffin saw a picture of his dad in a fit of rage, beating him with both fists as hard as he could as Griffin's mom rushed to pull him away. Griffin's mom was screaming at Griffin with her loud, piercing voice. She sounded so judgmental and condemning, totally out of character.

"God bless my mom," Griffin said.

Griffin's mom had to play the part of a faithful, subservient wife to avoid his dad's wrath. She had to do what was expected of her. But later she'd pull Griffin aside to apologize. She was much kinder and gentler than what she could show in front of Griffin's dad.

Griffin dreaded going home. Then he saw another picture in his mind of his parents showing him the door and kicking him out onto the streets. A paralyzing kind of fear ran through his entire body.

There'd be no speeding for Griffin this time. He had calmed down, but the opposite effect controlled his body. Griffin deliberately traveled slower than the speed limit, pretending he was *Merlin the Wizard* with the capability to slow time and maybe avoid his parents a little longer.

Maybe a car will hit me, and they'll take me to the ER.

Griffin kept driving.

Maybe a hot young blonde will pick me up and take me back to her place.

The large, bright orange sun had almost fallen from the sky. It was nearly dark when Griffin arrived at his house on South Oakenwald Avenue in Kenwood. He reluctantly pulled himself out of his car, closed the door behind him, opened the front gate, and walked the concrete up the seven steps that led to his front door.

Griffin stood in front of the dark green door, paralyzed with fear.

Here's where I go down in flames.

He pounded on the front door.

The door opened a few inches as Griffin saw her eyes peer through the crack.

When the door finally opened, he watched his mom reach out her arms as if Griffin had been resurrected from the dead. Griffin stood there without reacting. He could see the anguish of his mom's tears. The entire scene played in slow motion as if Merlin's time magic was still working.

"Griffin, what happened to you? Those bruises on your face look awful. Sweetheart, are you okay? Your dad and I have been worried sick about you," his mom said.

Disbelief was written all over his face. Griffin's lips didn't move.

Where's the wrath? No judgmental condemnation? She's worried about me. When did she start caring?

"Looks like you've got two black eyes. Let me take care of you," Griffin's mom said.

She reached her right hand up to Griffin's face to gently touch it. Griffin recoiled with pain.

"I'm so sorry. Your face looks painful. Come in. I heard about the terrible fight today at school. When you didn't come home at your usual time, your dad and I became worried."

Griffin sat on the front couch without saying any words.

She's acting weird. Why is she acting so loving and kind? Where's Dad?

"Say something, Sweetheart."

She continued to cry and held Griffin's hand as if she'd never let it go.

Griffin's dad's steps were heavy. He sounded like a 1000-pound gorilla pounding the pavement as he entered the living room. The room grew still and quiet. Griffin's dad stared at him and then spoke.

"Griffin, are you okay? Principal Jones called and said you got into a fight at school today. Then you show up at dark. We were worried sick about where you were."

Worried about me? When did you ever care about me?

"God, your face looks terrible," Griffin's dad said.

Thanks, Dad for noticing.

Griffin stood there with a puzzled look on his face. For once his dad seemed to genuinely care about him. Or was it all pretend? Would his face suddenly turn bright red and would his dad throw him on the floor and violently beat him.?

Proceed with caution, Griffin thought.

A yellow light flashed in front of Griffin.

Griffin stared at his dad. He was frozen in disbelief, unsure of how to answer him.

If he rushes me, I'm running for the door.

"I spoke to you, Son. Aren't you going to answer me?" his dad asked.

Silence.

"Griffin are you okay?" his dad asked again.

"No, I'm not, Dad. I just got the shit beat out of me," Griffin replied.

"I am so sorry, Son. Principal Jones called and said you got beat up. Then you didn't show till now. We were worried sick about you."

Worried about me? Griffin thought. *The gorilla's about to strike. I'm getting ready to run.*

Griffin's dad moved closer to him and stopped short of Griffin's face. He looked Griffin straight in the eye. Griffin was unsure of what his dad's intentions were. His dad waited for a response.

"Your mom and I are sorry you got beat up today at school," Griffin's dad said.

"Thank you," Griffin replied.

"What exactly happened?" his dad asked.

Dear God, what am I going to say?

"I thought I'd go in early to school so I could get some homework done. I was cornered in the hallway next to my locker. Some thugs lifted me off the floor and slammed me into the lockers."

"For no reason at all?" Griffin's dad interrupted.

"Yes, for no reason at all."

The room was calm and peaceful like before a storm.

Why do they need to have a reason to abuse me? Griffin thought.

"Oh, sweetheart, I am so sorry they did that to you," Griffin's mom said.

What's gotten into my mom? For once, she seemed to really care about me. Griffin waited in silence for more words to come. He thought about what his dad might say next.

"Griffin, you can't be a sissy. You've got to fight back and kick their asses," Griffin thought.

But his dad didn't say any of that. For once, his dad showed the kinder side of himself. For once, his dad supported him and took Griffin's side. Still, Griffin was optimistically cautious.

"Where are your glasses, Sweetheart?" Griffin's mom asked.

"They took them and grinded them into the tile floor," Griffin replied.

"Oh, poor baby, I'm so sorry," his mom said.

Wow, my mom has a heart, Griffin thought.

"What happened next?" Griffin's mom asked.

Griffin took a deep breath and exhaled slowly. Then he spoke.

"Those thugs spat in my face. Then they stuffed paper into my mouth, put duct tape over my lips, and dragged my body by my feet up the stairs to the second floor," Griffin answered.

"Animals, nothing but sick animals," Griffin's father shouted.

"You're right, Dad. They're animals," Griffin replied. "I tried to fight back and break free, but they held me by my arms and legs. I was outnumbered.

"Those sick animals are going to pay," Griffin's dad shouted.

Griffin's dad rose from his chair, his fists clenched tightly, randomly swinging them in the air. Mom coaxed him into taking a seat, calming him down like a professional trainer could gently calm a wild buck after a violent episode.

I'm running out that door, Griffin thought.

But instead Griffin stood there speechless. There was a long pause after his dad exhibited his intense anger. Then Griffin's mother spoke.

"Sweetheart, that is criminal what they did to you."

"I can't believe no one was around to protect you—not even the principal," Griffin's dad said.

I can't believe Mom and Dad are finally showing their love and support, Griffin thought.

"There's more. They dragged my body into the bathroom. Each one took turns punching and kicking me. I was scared they were going to rape me," Griffin said.

"Oh, Sweetheart, that is cruel and sick. And there were no teachers or security around?" his mom asked.

"No one was there to help me," he replied.

The room was filled with silence and shock.

"Animals, sick and rabid animals," Griffin's dad said.

I believe you just said that, Dad, Griffin thought.

The room grew incredibly quiet. Griffin trembled and stuttered with deep emotion. His mom and dad were stunned with disbelief. Griffin continued.

"They peed in the toilet bowl. Then they tied me by my feet with a long rope. They threw the other end over a steel ceiling pipe. Those thugs hoisted my body up by my feet and lowered my head into that disgusting bowl of yellow urine. They forced my head to go under the bowl of pee," he said.

Griffin's mom broke out in tears, sobbing and crying. Her head fell between her knees.

Griffin's father was past the point of boiling. He rose from his chair again like a madman who had just been locked in solitary confinement, randomly swinging his tightly clenched fists into mid-air.

"Wait till I get my hands on those bastards. I'm going to make them wish they had never laid a hand on you!" his dad said.

Please, God, don't let him hit me. Griffin hesitantly continued.

"They cut me down from the pipe and dragged me to the center of the bathroom. They both pissed on me like I was a worthless piece of trash."

"That is shameless!" Griffin's dad yelled out at the top of his voice.

Griffin paused for a few seconds. Tears were flowing down his face. He held his head low with anguish. Griffin's voice broke as he struggled to get the words out of his mouth.

"It's been difficult," Griffin confessed.

Griffin was sobbing but tried to hide it from his parents.

"I wasn't sure how to tell you and how you would take it," Griffin said.

"Oh, Honey, we are here for you," Griffin's mom said.

"Thank you, Mom."

"When did they find you?" Griffin's dad asked.

"Coach Jackson rushed into the bathroom and caught them in the act. He broke it up. He grabbed one of their arms and held him down. Seconds later, Principal Jones rushed in to hold down the other lowlife," Griffin replied.

"You are lucky to be alive," Griffin's mom said.

"If Coach Jackson hadn't come along, I don't know what they would've done to me. Maybe left me for dead," Griffin said.

"Oh, that is so awful. Just horrible," his mom said.

"Damn sick, if you ask me," his dad said.

"After they cleaned me up, Principal Jones ordered all of us into his office. The police escorted us. I needed a lot of help. I was so sore; I could barely walk," Griffin said.

"What happened next?" his father asked.

At that point, Griffin felt like he needed to leave the house. He could see his dad growing dangerously violent and knew he could absolutely snap at any time. But Griffin didn't go. For once, Griffin faced his fear. If his dad became violent, Griffin would stand up to him.

Griffin became quiet and speechless.

"Finish your story," Griffin's dad demanded.

He hesitantly continued. "Those thugs sat in the office surrounded by the police, security, and the teachers who rescued me."

"Did Principal Jones get to the bottom of it?" Griffin's dad asked.

"He questioned us for hours, but no one said a word," Griffin replied.

"Not even you?" his dad asked.

Here we go again, Dad's gonna explode, Griffin thought.

Griffin was slow to answer.

"No, not even me. I was afraid that they might kill me," Griffin replied

"I don't blame you. I would have been afraid too," Griffin's dad said.

Did he just say that? Unbelievable. Maybe my dad has a heart too.

"What happened next?" his dad asked.

"No one was about to talk or rat out each other, so Principal Jones expelled them. He said they were never welcomed back at school again, period," Griffin answered.

"Good. They damn well deserved it," Griffin's dad said.

Griffin's mom rushed toward him and held Griffin tightly in her arms, rocking him as if he were two years old again.

Griffin's father paced the floor, shaking his fists angrily at the ceiling.

"That's it, Griffin, that's it. Your mother and I are pulling you out of that hellhole school. You're never going back there again—ever. You'll finish school, even if we have to teach you ourselves."

CHAPTER FOUR

TOO MUCH TIME ON MY HANDS

December 14 was the date Griffin would always remember. The very last sentence, the closing chapter, and the words, "The end," all made him smile and want to rise from his chair to do the happy dance. Griffin could finally put *A Novel Life* to rest. Griffin clicked the save button with his mouse and all 59,127 words were etched on the hard drive on his Word document app, waiting for the day he would send it to publishers.

Pop the cork and stretch a big banner across the room that says, "I'M PROUD OF YOU GRIFFIN!" Play some funky dance music and invite your friends to celebrate this glorious moment. You've finally finished your first novel, Griffin thought.

Caps and gowns of the graduation that never happened, being slammed against the lockers in the hallway, hanging over the toilet bowl, and being pulled out of his own school by his parents were almost erased from Griffin's mind. The revenge plans he had pictured for his savage attackers were almost forgotten. He was totally lost in his little world of Griffin and the manuscript. Could writing have been his best therapy? How could he have totally forgotten about all the deep-seated anger built up inside of him? Is it possible that all his deep anger and wrath vanished? Or would it return, only to haunt him and cause him to later commit heinous crimes? Those were questions Griffin asked himself repeatedly.

Griffin started reading articles from the *pros* who suggested that if he were to submit a manuscript to a publisher, it would be wise to ask an English teacher or a published author to edit it before he was to submit it for publication. So, he went online and researched editors in Chicago. There were plenty of editors to choose from in his Google search. Griffin wasn't sure if they were part of a scam or if they were legitimate. Many of them charged steep prices to edit manuscripts—particularly a manuscript with over 50,000 words.

God, I'm a poor dropout student who's got no money. Give me a break, Griffin thought

Griffin could have asked the English teacher at his old school, but he didn't want to go there. He had too many painful memories. Finally, he found a friend of a friend whose dad was a published author. This man was an English teacher at the local community college, which was only three miles from where Griffin lived. Griffin sent him an email and explained to him how he had finished his debut novel and was interested in getting it published. He thought it was worth a shot to try this teacher since he came highly recommended, but Griffin wasn't sure if the teacher would reply since he was a very busy man.

About a week later, the English professor, Mr. Martin from the City College of Chicago, replied to his email. Mr. Martin was very supportive, enthusiastic, and understood that Griffin was a seventeen-year-old kid with no money. He agreed to help Griffin. Mr. Martin asked Griffin to meet him at the college and to bring the completed manuscript. Mr. Martin agreed to only charge Griffin what he could afford to pay. Griffin did have a small savings account and felt it would be nice to pay Mr. Martin something for his services.

It would also be a good investment to have a fully edited manuscript. Griffin could go far with a polished manuscript. Perhaps, he could get the attention of a big publisher and land a deal. And he could even go to the top of the *New York Times* bestselling list.

Mr. Martin fit the stereotyped look of a college English teacher to a T. He was medium height with dark brown hair, a moustache and beard. He wore wire-rimmed glasses and dressed in a brown corduroy sports coat with a bright yellow bowtie. Griffin couldn't see the top of his office desk because it was buried deep under the piles of papers and books.

"Here it is," Griffin said.

Griffin proudly handed over his manuscript sealed in a large manila envelope.

"I know you're proud of this. That's quite an accomplishment for someone your age," Mr. Martin replied.

"You bet I am," Griffin replied.

"I know you must've worked hard on this." Mr. Martin said.

"I did. I am grateful I had a lot of time to finish it," Griffin said.

"Well, you know I will give it my utmost care. I will give it my best in editing," Mr. Martin said.

"Thank you, Sir."

"You're welcome. I will try my best to get it back to you before the new year," Mr. Martin said.

He seems honest and sincere. Maybe he will really help me, Griffin thought.

Griffin was excited that a published author and a college English teacher was mentoring him. He felt cared for. For the first time in a long time, someone believed in him. Griffin passed the time away for the next couple of December weeks by researching book publishers online and reading a book he found at the library, *Writer's Digest for Authors*. Griffin found it curious that about half of the major book publishers accepted unsolicited material, without needing an agent, and about half required an agent to shop a manuscript.

Griffin decided to shop his manuscript without the assistance of an agent. He was impatient. Getting a book deal through an agent would take far too long.

By the time that agent was to get me a contract I would be thirty years old. Sure, the agent might be able to get me a hefty advance, but I would waste nearly thirteen years of my life trying to get one book deal, Griffin thought.

***

January fifth finally came. Hopefully, it would be a much better year than the last. Griffin was pumped because Mr. Martin called him to tell him his manuscript was completely edited.

"You are one gifted writer," Mr. Martin said.

Griffin was taken back by his words. He was speechless.

"You have an original, fresh story. Your writing is impeccable," Mr. Martin said.

"Thank you," Griffin replied with a humble-sounding voice.

Griffin was nervous, stumbling over his own words.

"I couldn't find a whole lot of things wrong with your manuscript. I changed some punctuation, some paragraph spacing and a few word choices. You are a naturally gifted writer. You don't see those too often."

Is this dude for real? Is he just telling me what I want to hear or does he really think I have talent?

"Do you really think I'm a naturally gifted writer?" Griffin asked.

"Look, kid, I wouldn't lie to you. I speak the truth from my heart and with experience. I have seen a lot of hack amateur writers in my days. But I've only seen a handful of naturally gifted writers like you. I count them on my fingers; that's how rare they are," Mr. Martin replied.

"Thank you, Sir."

His words seem sincere. That makes me very happy, Griffin thought.

"Pay me whatever you can afford. Let's say $100 and call it a day."

Griffin was flabbergasted. *Only $100 for all that work?*

"Okay, if you say so. Thank you for your kind words and help," Griffin said.

"You're welcome. I believe you've got a hit on your hands—a bestselling novel. You're definitely going places, young man," Mr. Martin said.

He didn't have to say those kind words. In fact, he didn't have to say anything. But he did, Griffin thought.

Griffin was ecstatic. He was so excited that he was ready to send his manuscript to whoever would read it and possibly consider publishing it.

Griffin knew he still had more work to do. As hard as it was for him, he had to be patient.

***

I will always remember that day when Mr. Martin took the time to mentor me. I will never forget Mr. Martin's generosity and kindness. I ended the chapter with fond memories of him. Cheers to you, Mr. Martin.

CHAPTER FIVE
HURRY UP AND WAIT

"God, someone spare me from this torture. This is not what I signed up for," Griffin said to himself.

Editing and re-writing wasn't Griffin's favorite thing to do. He would have rather been fishing, driving his car, hiking, or writing another novel. No one was cracking his back with a whip nor was anyone twisting his arm or mouthing off words at the top of their lungs, ordering him around. But Griffin knew if he was going to be published and be successful at it, this is what he would have to do to get to the top. So, the rest of January was spent checking every word, every sentence, and every paragraph backwards and forward until it was perfect.

They call that editing and proofing. I call it hell, Griffin thought.

Of course, Griffin had to be born a perfectionist. It was in his DNA. Griffin's father was a perfectionist; his aunt and grandmother were also born that way. So naturally Griffin wanted his manuscript to be just right—perfect. Griffin felt that if he had it down perfect, he would have a better shot at getting someone to publish it.

Griffin's parents knew what he was doing, but he had the impression they thought he was wasting his time, writing frantically for hours in his room and trying to *chase a dream.* They worried about Griffin and his future. He'd be rich if he got a dollar for every time they told him to finish school and get a real job. But Griffin didn't listen to them. He believed in himself and was convinced he would become a *New York Times* bestselling author if not now, one day. Going to college to get a, "real job," was the last thing on his mind.

I wish they would get over it.

Griffin finally finished his manuscript on the first day of February, and it was, "publisher ready." Every dot was placed in the right place, every T was crossed, and every quote and punctuation were correct. Griffin was stoked. He was ready to change the world with his new novel, *A Novel Life*. All week, he prepared query letters and carefully followed the publisher's instructions on how to submit. Griffin sent his first chapter with a query letter to all the publishers who required electronic submissions through email. Next, he bought twelve large manila envelopes, addressed each one, and printed his query letters with book proposals to each acquisition editor. Griffin printed copies of the first chapter of his new novel. Papers and envelopes were strewn everywhere. It looked like a twister had hit his room. Griffin enclosed each copy of the first chapter into an envelope with a copy of his query letter and proposal. He carefully sealed each envelope. On Friday of that week, Griffin walked with his head held high. Each step his Converses took him on the sidewalk made him feel like a new man. Griffin was on his way to the post office, a few blocks from his house. He stood in line with a big smile on his face and waited. When it was his turn, Griffin stepped up to the counter with his shoulders and chin held high.

"How many have you got?" the postal clerk asked.

"Twelve," Griffin replied.

She weighed each one, asked him if he had any dangerous substances or chemicals in them, and stamped them all.

"That will be $39.60."

Griffin reached into his pocket, pulled out two twenty-dollar bills, and handed them to her.

"This is my very first novel I'm sending to publishers," he said.

The clerk acted as if she couldn't care less. Her eyes were halfway reading a text message on her phone, which she held in one hand, while she handed Griffin change of forty cents with a receipt. Worst of all, she didn't even answer him—never opened her mouth once. Griffin could tell she was more interested in taking her lunch break than talking to him.

She doesn't care about me. God, I wish I had some friends I could share my feelings with. It gets lonely sometimes.

Griffin turned away and mumbled, "Thanks for nothing." As each foot hit the sidewalk, taking him one step closer to his house, Griffin thought about what happened.

I'm not going to let some clerk ruin my day. What does she know about writing books? She's probably never read a book in her life, much less written one.

Griffin was pumped. He was proud of himself for what he had accomplished. He had written an entire 59,127-word novel in three months. His novel was on its way to twelve book publishers.

Someone's got to love it, Griffin thought

The February snowstorms changed into windy March days. Those chilly windy March days turned into an early April spring, and now it was the first week of June. Griffin stayed awake in his bed every night during those four months worrying about his manuscript.

Damn publishers. Why haven't I heard from them? I guess they don't care, Griffin thought.

Griffin had worked countless hours to finish his manuscript to perfection. He had rushed to get it all done by January. He worked so hard to get his manuscripts into the hands of those publishers by February and there was not one response—not even a rejection letter.

Griffin's parents were putting enormous pressure on him to get a job. They would read the classified job listings in the *Chicago Tribune* every morning at breakfast.

"If you're not going to get your GED and go to college, at least get a job," Griffin's dad said with a judgmental tone in his voice.

"It's summer, Griffin, it's a good time to get a job," his mom said.

Griffin got tired of hearing all their nagging. It was wearing on him It was as painful as being stuck on the, "Small World," ride at Disney World and having to hear the tune play a thousand times continuously.

So, Griffin applied for a few jobs advertised on Craigslist. They were mostly dull, boring jobs, but they did pay money. And he was short of money.

A few weeks later, Griffin got hired as a department assistant at Home Depot. It was a ho-hum job, but it did give him some extra money.

June dragged on into July. Griffin was knee-deep in boredom. He had completely forgotten about those publishers. They were the furthest things from his mind.

What am I going to do with my life if I can't be an author? Griffin thought.

July 30 was a monumental day; one Griffin would always remember. Griffin arrived home from work, tired as he could be, and reached inside the mailbox. Soon his life would change forever.

***

I remember working my butt off writing my book, preparing query letters, and pitching the manuscript. I wasn't sure if that day would ever come or if I would only dream of being an author for the rest of my life.

31

CHAPTER SIX
MY LIFE CHANGED FOREVER

Today was a miracle, one amazing miracle. The news arrived at the very moment Griffin needed it.

Griffin was at the point in his life where he felt like a worthless bag of garbage being discarded at the bottom of a dumpster beside some lonely unforgotten warehouse. Griffin heard the words every day from his parents, "Griffin, when are you going to actually do something with your life?"

Griffin guessed they thought all those times he was working hard on his novel, stowed away inside his room that he was smoking Mexican street weed, having wild orgies with whores, and downing fifths of Jack Daniels while strung out across his bed, wasted away in Griffin Ville.

Griffin was exhausted from lifting bags of mulch and manure for customers. He headed home, parked his car by the curb, and reached his hand inside the mailbox as he usually did when he came home. He didn't pay much attention to the mail he held in his hands. Griffin opened the front door and followed his feet where they led him, up the stairs to his room. He threw the mail down on his desk, knowing he would eventually turn it over to his parents. There was probably nothing important. He was sprawled out in his chair, staring at the ceiling fan whirling around above his head. Griffin was trying to rid his mind of its inner demons. He looked down and his eyes caught an important-looking letter scattered on his desk. It was addressed to him, "Mr. Griffin Smith."

How strange, no one ever writes me a letter, and no one addresses it to me with mister, Griffin thought.

Griffin tore open the envelope like some rabid madman in a frenzy.

The letter was signed by Arnold Turnbull, Chief Editor for Sheldon House Publishers. It was earth-shattering. Someone loved his manuscript and wanted to publish it. Not only did someone want to publish it, that someone was the Chief Editor of the top publishing house in New York—Sheldon House. Mr. Turnbull had a reputation for being one of the most influential decision makers in the history of publishing. Besides, Sheldon House had more *New York Times* bestsellers than any other publishers.

Griffin felt like a rocket that had just been launched. He was riding high like a satellite orbiting the Earth. Memories of his rejection letters from other publishers faded from his mind. All his troubles seemed to disappear for the moment. Being beaten up nearly every day at that crappy school, being pulled out of school in his senior year, worrying about finding a job, and having to deal with his parents harassing him every day became distant memories left behind on an old dirt road somewhere far from here. All Griffin could think of was signing a publishing deal and his promising future of writing books for Sheldon House and Mr. Turnbull.

The sentences stood out in the letter like a drop-dead, knock-out, gorgeous girl stands out in a crowd.

The letter read:

> *You are a gifted author. We love how you developed your characters and how mature your writing is for your age. You are a natural. We look forward to working together with you.*
>
> *Please call me at your earliest convenience. We at Sheldon House wish to meet with you as soon as possible about your manuscript.*
> *Sincerely, Mr. Arnold Turnbull.*

Griffin wasted no time. He didn't even take time to share the news with his parents. He ran to his room and picked up his phone to dial the number. It was still only four p.m. in New York City, and it was possible to reach someone at the company.

"Sheldon House Publishers, how may I help you?" the receptionist asked.

"I am calling for Mr. Arnold Turnbull," Griffin said.

"May I ask who's calling?" the receptionist asked.

"This, this, this... is... Griffin Smith."

"Just a minute, I'll see if Mr. Turnbull is available," she replied.

The phone went dead—no crappy recorded message and no sucky music. All Griffin could hear was the gum cracking and popping in his mouth.

The silence was broken with a very deep, authoritative, commanding voice.

"Arnold Turnbull speaking."

Griffin's legs were shaking like a washer shakes with an uneven load, and his stomach was doing triple somersaults. Griffin could barely breathe, like someone had held a pillow over his face.

"Mr. Turnbull, this is Griff... Griff...Griffin Smith," Griffin said.

The phone went silent.

"Oh, yes, Griffin Smith. Griffin, my young lad, how are you?" Mr. Turnbull asked.

"Sto-o-o-ked," Griffin replied.

"You should be. I personally read your manuscript *A Novel Life*. It's a masterpiece and a hit at that. It's the best novel since *Forest Gump*. It is mature and beyond your years. It's simply marvelous. Are you really eighteen? Turnbull asked.

"Barely eighteen," Griffin replied.

"It's rare to find a manuscript as great as yours particularly from the writer himself and not through an agent. Most of our submissions come through agents. But since we do accept material from outside writers without agents, we occasionally find a marvelous writer like you," Mr. Turnbull said

"Thanks," Griffin answered.

"Let's talk about what comes next for you. We want to offer you a contract," Turnbull said.

"Awesome," Griffin replied.

"How soon can you fly to New York?" Turnbull asked.

"Today, if you'd like, sir."

Mr. Turnbull roared with laughter over Griffin's naive and zealous answer.

"Could you meet with me this Friday at two p.m. Eastern time? We'll send you airline tickets, and all of your expenses will be paid for while you're here," Mr. Turnbull said.

"Okay, I'll be there, Friday at two p.m.," Griffin replied.

"Marvelous, Griffin. I'll buy your ticket, and you'll have it today. I'll email you info on where you'll be staying and arrange a taxi to pick you up at LaGuardia. I still can't get over your book. It's simply marvelous. Marvelous. See you soon," Mr. Turnbull said.

Keep on saying 'marvelous' as many times as you'd like, Griffin thought.

"Okay, thanks Mr. Turnbull," Griffin said.

Griffin nearly tripped over his feet as he hung up the phone and rushed downstairs to tell his mom the news. Finally, this news would be Griffin's sweet, ultimate revenge against those lowlife bullies. Ever since the day he spent by the river after being brutally beaten, Griffin vowed to take the high road and be bigger than those bullies. If only he had some friends to tell the good news to.

Griffin shouted to his mom and dad with all his might, "I'm flying to New York on Friday!"

***

I would learn later how delighted Mr. Turnbull was to discover me. Mr. Turnbull was even more excited to meet me. I discovered that I meant more to Turnbull than merely being an author. Turnbull saw big-bucks dollar signs in me. I could put Turnbull back on the *New York Times* bestselling list. Turnbull missed not being at the center of attention. I learned later how much Mr. Turnbull had missed his glory days on the top of the bestselling list. Ten years had been way too long. Turnbull couldn't rest on his laurels anymore. It was time to get back in the game again. Turnbull thought I might just put him back on top.

I was riding high, on top of the world, or at least I thought so.

CHAPTER SEVEN
NEW YORK, HERE I COME!

"New York, here I come," Griffin said to himself.

Griffin spoke so loudly everyone on the plane heard him.

Griffin chewed the skin off his fingernails with his mouth and changed his seating position perhaps fifty times in row 9A. It was good that no one was sitting next to him. Griffin would have driven that person crazy with his basket of nerves. Through his dazed stare out the window, Griffin could see the airport traffic controller carefully directing the plane. The Boeing 737 was moving in reverse away from the hanger of Midway Airport. Griffin felt the plane turn and stop, awaiting the signal to taxi down the runway. It was 10:15 a.m. CST as the wheels lifted off the ground and the plane shot straight toward the sky at an almost forty-five-degree angle.

Griffin took a deep breath as he heard the landing gear disengage.

I can't believe it's all coming true, Griffin thought.

Barring no emergencies or delays, Griffin would arrive in LaGuardia Airport at 1:15 p.m. EST. His exciting new adventure was about to come true in New York. It gave a whole new meaning to the phrase, "Thank God, it's Friday."

In his mind, Griffin was holding that VIP letter in his hands. That scene was repeated over and over in his head. To think that only eighty-nine hours ago, the amazing and great Editor-in-Chief of the top publishing company, Sheldon House, Mr. Arnold Turnbull was congratulating him for his soon-to-be bestselling novel, and he had invited him to New York for a VIP meeting. Now Griffin was on the plane headed to meet him in person, courtesy of Sheldon House—all expenses paid.

My parents can't stop me, even if they tried, Griffin thought.

Griffin was barely eighteen, but he felt like he had been an adult for years. He was on his own and could fly to New York for the meeting without anyone telling him he couldn't. But, fortunately, his parents were supportive enough when they found out about his contract offer with perhaps the biggest and best publisher in the world. They were proud of him, and all the preachy past talk of getting a, "real job," became mute.

Griffin passed the time by listening to his faves list on Spotify. Still it was hard to focus on the songs. All his mind could think of was his meeting with Mr. Turnbull. He was so stoked that he couldn't stand it. In less than four and a half hours, Mr. Turnbull would be offering him a contract for his first book.

Griffin was deep in thought.

"Sir, what would you like to drink?" the flight attendant asked.

She only heard silence. Griffin didn't hear her.

"Sir, what would you like to drink?" the attendant asked again.

"Oh, sorry," Griffin replied, his mind catching up.

She looked at Griffin and waited for his answer

"Give me a Coke, please," Griffin said.

"Got it," the attendant said.

Griffin put his buds in his phone and listened to some more songs. The attendant brought him a Coke and a small bag of pretzels.

"Thank you," he said.

The trip passed quickly while listening to his playlist, munching on pretzels, and downing the Coke.

Griffin felt someone tap him on the shoulder. He removed his buds and heard the Captain's voice.

"This is your Captain speaking. We are preparing to land in LaGuardia in about five minutes. We are descending. Please remain seated with your seatbelts on, your seats upright, and your trays put away. Put your phone, laptops, and tablets in airplane mode until we land. Thank you for your cooperation."

The plane quickly descended. Griffin heard the wheels engage and he could see Lady Liberty proudly smiling and applauding him. Griffin knew it wouldn't be long before his plane landed. He felt like he was holding the winning lottery ticket to the Power Ball. Griffin was going to collect his forty million dollars. Then he felt the wheels of the plane touch the runway. They had landed. He was about to experience an adventure of a lifetime in New York.

He grabbed his bag, pushing and shoving his way through the crowd. Griffin felt his newly found freedom when he stepped off the plane. As he entered the gigantic, crowded terminal, his eyes caught a glimpse of a tall, well-dressed man holding a large neon-colored sign with Griffin's name on it. He was dressed in a gray, pin-striped, three-piece suit. His dark-brown hair was neatly trimmed, and he wore sunglasses. The man could have been a double for a secret service agent. He and his sign were easy to spot in the crowd. Griffin rushed toward him.

"I'm Griffin Smith."

"ID please," the man replied.

Griffin reached into his rear pants pocket, pulled out his wallet, lifted his Illinois Driver's License and handed it to him.

"That will do it," he said as he handed Griffin his license back.

Griffin put his license and wallet back into his pocket.

"Follow me," the man said.

Griffin followed him to the transportation area outside of the terminal. The man took his bag and placed it in the trunk of a long black limousine. He opened the rear passenger door as Griffin stepped inside. He couldn't believe it. He was traveling in style. He was headed to 1717 Avenue of the Americas, which was located near Central Park. Griffin felt like the most important person in the world.

CHAPTER EIGHT
THE MILLION DOLLAR MEETING

Excitement overtook Griffin and captured him like the moment someone tells you you've won 400 million in the jackpot lottery.

It was early, only 1:45 p.m., when Griffin arrived at 1717 Avenue of the Americas. The limousine pulled in front of the tall, ornate concrete building located across the street from Central Park.

"We're here," the limousine driver said.

He opened his driver's door, walked around to Griffin's side door and opened it to let him out.

"Good luck with your meeting today," the driver said.

"Thanks," Griffin replied.

"Oh, and go to the 23rd floor. Mr. Turnbull will be waiting," he said as he closed Griffin's passenger side door.

Wow, what service, Griffin thought.

Griffin grabbed his bag and stepped inside the marbled-floor lobby through the large brass-covered glass doors.

The guard and receptionist at the marbled counter asked for Griffin's ID and whom he was here to see.

"I have a two o'clock meeting with Mr. Arnold Turnbull of Sheldon House," Griffin answered.

The receptionist called the 23rd floor to confirm Griffin's appointment.

There was a pause of silence while he waited.

"Okay, you're good to go. Mr. Turnbull is expecting you," the receptionist said.

"Thanks," Griffin replied.

"Take the elevator around the corner to the 23rd floor," the guard said.

"Got it," Griffin replied.

Griffin took about forty steps from the counter and around the corner until he found the elevator. He pushed the up arrow. After waiting a few minutes, the brass-covered elevator doors opened, and Griffin stepped in. Men and women were dressed in Armani suits, gold bracelets, gold Rolex watches, and one thousand-dollar neckties. Griffin couldn't breathe. The elevator was stuffed like a pack of sardines squeezed into one can. People were texting, making phone conversations, and were buried into the *New York Times*. Griffin struggled to reach his arm through the crowd to push the 23rd floor button. Everyone was inside their own little world. No one said a word to him. In fact, Griffin could've been the ant crawling on the side of the elevator wall or a ghost. No one saw him enter or leave that elevator. They were too busy.

The elevator stopped on the 23rd floor, the door opened, and Griffin shoved his way out and into the hallway where he couldn't miss seeing the large gold sign of the logo, Sheldon House Publishers. It was clearly visible through the all-glass doors and windows of the offices. Griffin opened the large, beveled-glass door and stepped up to the long marble receptionist's desk.

"May I help you?" the receptionist asked.

"I have a two o'clock meeting with Mr. Turnbull," Griffin replied.

"Your name please," the receptionist said.

"Griffin Smith."

The receptionist called Mr. Turnbull. Griffin waited.

"Mr. Turnbull is expecting you. Please have a seat. He will be with you shortly. Could I get you something to drink: water, soda, coffee?" the receptionist asked.

"Sure, I'd like a Coke please," Griffin replied.

Griffin sat himself down on one of the marble benches positioned in the waiting area around the large glass windows. He tried to make himself comfortable, but the benches were too hard. Griffin was about seven minutes early. He fidgeted nervously, between checking his phone and messing with his hair. Griffin was so nervous that his legs were shaking.

The clock on his phone read two o'clock. Griffin's heart raced quickly. He could feel the adrenaline rush through every ounce of his body. Griffin was a wreck. Any minute now, he would face one of the most powerful men in the book publishing business.

Two o'clock passed. Griffin nervously waited. He fidgeted some more. He stood up and nervously paced the floor. His phone read two seventeen p.m.

What had happened? Did he forget about me? Maybe he changed his mind, Griffin thought.

Just when Griffin was ready to ask the receptionist about Mr. Turnbull, she called his name. The fog had lifted. It was safe to finally breathe again.

"Mr. Smith, Mr. Turnbull is ready to see you," the receptionist said.

Griffin wasn't used to being addressed as a mister. He nervously followed the receptionist to the rear area of the office. She opened a large, gold-covered glass door as he entered.

A long mahogany table was positioned in the center of the room. Men and women dressed in million-dollar suits with ties sat at the table. Griffin sheepishly walked toward the table with his head and shoulders slumped.

A tall determined-looking man dressed in a silk, pin-striped looking suit stood in front of Griffin and offered him his hand to shake.

"I'm Arnold Turnbull," he said with a deep, strong authoritative voice.

Griffin paused a second, trying to pull himself together.

You can do it, Griffin. Give it your best shot, Griffin thought.

"I'm Griffin Smith," he said meekly.

"We're glad you're here," Mr. Turnbull replied.

The room was quiet enough to make a crying baby sleep. But Griffin's knees shook with fear. He tried not to let it show.

God, this is intimidation at its best, Griffin thought.

"Have a seat," Mr. Turnbull said as he pointed to a vacant chair at the boardroom table.

Griffin seated himself much like Frankenstein would have and halfway smiled at Turnbull.

Mr. Turnbull began introducing Griffin to the neatly dressed men and women seated at the table. They were all his staff members and the Sheldon House Publishing team. Griffin couldn't have remembered their names even if he had tried. They were all strangers. He was in a strange city, strange building, seated among perfect strangers.

What am I doing here? What are you about to get yourself into, Griffin? Griffin thought.

Griffin's mind suddenly flashed back to his final day at William Fentress High when the principal had seated everyone in his office after the brutal beating Griffin had received in the men's bathroom. The horrendous scene where Griffin was almost raped still followed him like a ghost of the past. Griffin kept his hands hidden under the conference table because the palm of his hands began to sweat profusely thinking of that day he was severely beaten by those thugs.

Griffin stared at Mr. Turnbull as he began to talk. He was nothing like the Editor-in-Chief Griffin had imagined him to be. Turnbull looked to be about fiftyish. He had a full head of short hair—gray and black mixed. He wore narrow, wire-rimmed glasses and had a moustache and goatee which were both black with a touch of gray. Turnbull crossed his arms when he spoke, giving the appearance of a very powerful figure. Griffin noticed that he seldom smiled.

***

Mr. Turnbull studied Griffin's face, body language, and words carefully. Griffin could tell Turnbull was curious about him. This is how Turnbull imagined Griffin would look. Turnbull's eyes gave himself away as he studied Griffin's face. Turnbull acted as if he had seen a ghost. Griffin's appearance was exactly how Mr. Turnbull thought he would be.

43

"Mr. Smith, we absolutely love your new novel," Mr. Turnbull said.

Griffin acknowledged Turnbull's compliment by shaking his head without saying a word. Griffin's knees continued to tremble uncontrollably.

"It's brilliant. It's clever. It is a masterpiece. Most of all, it's a hit," Turnbull said.

***

And marvelous. But he didn't say the word, Griffin thought.

Griffin's lips were glued together. He forced a nervous smile of approval.

"We are prepared to offer you a contract," Turnbull said.

Get up and do the happy dance, Griffin, Griffin thought. Again, Griffin shook his head with approval but remained quiet.

"This book will definitely go to the top of the *New York Times* bestselling list," Turnbull said.

Griffin bit his tongue and held back his words even though he wanted to shout with joy and do the happy dance right then and there.

"We're prepared to offer you an advance of $100,000. This is unheard of for a first-time author. But, since your book will sell millions of copies, we are comfortable offering you this advance," Turnbull said.

At that point, Griffin couldn't hold back any longer. Turnbull was offering Griffin an advance of $100,000. That was a whole lot of money to Griffin. Griffin pictured in his mind fast cars, hot motorcycles, stylish clothes, exotic trips, lavish parties; everything money could buy.

Go ahead and say it, Griffin. You can do it, Griffin thought.

"I accept your offer," Griffin said as he raised his voice.

"Marvelous," Mr. Turnbull replied.

Griffin watched Mr. Turnbull eyes suddenly light up like a million stars. Griffin's lips were glued together. He forced a nervous smile of approval.

44

There he goes, using his favorite word, marvelous, Griffin thought.

Griffin smiled at him with approval.

"By the way, you can call me Griffin," Griffin said.

"Okay, Griffin. But there's more. We are launching a spectacular, sixty-city book tour starting next fall. The release date of your book is September fifteenth of next year," Turnbull said.

"Wow, a sixty-city book tour. It sounds exciting," Griffin replied.

"It will be a marvelous adventure. You will start in Chicago, your hometown, and travel to many of the towns and cities in the U.S. You will cover most of the bookstores, and some other venues," Turnbull said.

"How long will all that take?" Griffin asked.

"You will be on the road for at least six months traveling from city to city. We will pay all of your expenses," Turnbull continued.

"What will I be doing at each book signing?" Griffin asked.

"Well, for starters, you'll be reading some excerpts from your book. You will be answering questions from the audiences on you and your book. Each book event will end with a meet and greet reception for your audiences. You will not only be signing at books stores, but at other venues. And, of course, you will be personally signing each book for fans," Turnbull replied.

"Wow sounds like a lot of fun, but a whole lot of work," Griffin said.

"Oh, it will be marvelous, but I am sure you won't have any problem with hard work; will you, Griffin?" Turnbull asked.

He doesn't know what a hard worker I am, Griffin thought.

"No, sir," Griffin replied.

"Good. There is some work expected on your end. We will be editing your novel and will expect you to proofread your book at least three times. You might want to get some additional help from a professional such as an English teacher or journalist," Turnbull said.

"Sounds overwhelming," Griffin said.

"It is a tall task for anyone to accomplish in one year. How old will you be next fall, Griffin?" Turnbull asked.

"I will be nineteen," Griffin replied.

"So, you're eighteen now?" Turnbull asked.

"Yes, I just turned eighteen," Griffin answered.

Griffin shook his head and smiled, acknowledging Turnbull.

"If anyone can do it, you can. You'll even have your own publicist and manager to keep you on track," Turnbull said.

***

But I discovered later that Mr. Turnbull knew differently. Turnbull knew how much I could take and what the outcome would be on my book tour.

***

"Wow, it's really going to happen," Griffin said.

"You bet, Griffin. You're going to be famous once we're through with you," Turnbull said.

"By famous you mean like as in a household word?" Griffin asked.

"Yes, everyone will know you as an author like everyone knows Judy Blume, James Patterson, and John Grisham. We plan to launch a major publicity campaign with advertisements.

"Where will you advertise?" Griffin asked.

"Everywhere," Turnbull answered.

"Seriously?" Griffin asked.

At that moment, Turnbull told Griffin what he wanted to hear, not what Turnbull could see up ahead in Griffin's future.

"Seriously. Your book is the book of the century—that's how great it is, simply marvelous."

Griffin's mouth grew silent. His lips wouldn't move. He was speechless. Griffin sat for a moment and reflected on the words Mr. Turnbull had just told him. It was overwhelming. It was too much to take in all at once. Talk about one humbling experience.

"Now let's talk about the contract," Turnbull said.

Griffin stared as Turnbull handed him a large stack of what appeared to be paperwork from across the table. It looked like a thousand sheets of paper.

"There are two copies of the contract. I don't expect you to sign today. But I do expect you to keep your word that you will sign with Sheldon House. Have your attorney look over the contracts. Keep one copy for yourself and mail me your signed copy as soon as possible. I have signed both copies," Turnbull said.

"Will do," Griffin replied.

"Oh, and the check, I almost forgot," Turnbull said.

Mr. Turnbull held up a long green banker's check with the words Griffin Smith typed on it. The amount on the check was $100,000.

Griffin's eyes grew extra wide. He almost choked on his own saliva when he saw the amount.

"This check will be yours as soon as you sign the contracts and send one copy back to me," Turnbull said.

Mr. Turnbull was a smart, shrewd businessman. He was going to make Griffin wait until he sent the signed contract back, and then he'd give Griffin the money.

"I want to point out that the hundred grand is not a gift. It is not free money. It is an advance against your future royalties. You still have to pay taxes on it," Turnbull said.

"Could you explain how the advance works?" Griffin asked.

"Of course. Sheldon gives you a $100,000 advance. The first year your book sells one million copies, you are paid ten percent of the wholesale price of your book. The hardback copies sell for $24.95."

"How much is the wholesale price?" Griffin asked.

"Hold on, Griffin, and I will tell you. The wholesale price is half of the retail. So roughly you will be paid ten percent of about $12.50. That is almost $1.25 per book that you would receive," Turnbull answered.

"That doesn't sound like much," Griffin replied.

"It doesn't sound like a lot of money until you multiply it by one million. When you multiply $1.25 by one million sales you get 1.25 million."

"Wow, that's a whole lot of money," Griffin said.

"You better believe it's a whole lot of money. We're going to invest a whole lot of time and money into your book. It won't be easy, but we will take it to the top," Turnbull said.

"So how much would I get to keep?" Griffin asked.

"Well, the advance of $100,000 would be deducted from your 1.25 million. Which means you would still be able to keep $1,150,000. But remember, Griffin you'll have to pay a lot of taxes on that amount. By the time the government gets through with you, you'll be lucky to keep perhaps half of that—$550,000," Mr. Turnbull replied.

"Wow, that's a lot to give to the government," Griffin replied.

"You're not kidding. That is a lot. But look what you get to keep, $550,000. That's not too shabby for a kid who will be only nineteen," Turnbull said.

Griffin's head was spinning around and around, like the giant Ferris wheel you see in a carnival. He hadn't eaten lunch, and all the information Mr. Turnbull was throwing at him was overwhelming. Griffin wanted to scream, but in a good way. He couldn't believe a year from now, not only would he become famous, but he'd almost be a millionaire.

How is this possible? Griffin thought.

Griffin sat there in silence for a moment contemplating his next move. He was lost in thought. He could barely hear the words of Mr. Turnbull. Griffin was totally zoned out.

"Griffin, do we have a deal?" Turnbull asked.

"Oh, uh, uh, yes, of course," Griffin replied as if he had just awoken from a very deep sleep.

"Do you have any more questions to ask me or the staff members?" Turnbull asked.

"Yes, how do I dress when I'm on this book tour?" Griffin asked innocently.

Everyone, including Mr. Turnbull, roared with laughter. Then silence set in.

"You dress like you normally do, Griffin," Turnbull replied.

"No suits and ties?" Griffin asked.

"No suits and ties. The audiences who will be attending your book events want to see you as who you are—Griffin Smith, the nineteen-year-old author. Don't wear cut-off shorts or T-shirts, but wear jeans and a nice short sleeve shirt. They aren't expecting to meet a CEO or executive of some corporation. You are a nineteen-year-old for God's sake," Mr. Turnbull replied.

Mr. Turnbull is more down-to-earth than I thought. He's really a cool dude in disguise.

"You mean eighteen-year-old," Griffin said sheepishly.

"You know what I mean, Griffin," Turnbull said.

Griffin chuckled at his humor.

"Anything else?" Turnbull asked.

"Yes, how long will I be staying in New York? Will I get to see anything while I'm here?" Griffin asked.

"We've arranged for you to stay here until Monday. That means you have two and half more days to do anything you'd like. We'd like for you to enjoy your stay on us while you're here," Turnbull replied.

"How do I pay for things?" Griffin asked.

"Glad you asked. Here's some spending money to do with as you please," Mr. Turnbull said as he handed Griffin an envelope filled with cash.

"Oh, okay, thanks," Griffin said.

Griffin placed the envelope underneath the table so no one could see he was counting the money inside. He couldn't believe it, there was more than two thousand in cash.

"Does the amount meet with your approval?" Mr. Turnbull asked.

"Yes," Griffin replied sheepishly.

Two thousand cash to spend in two days. That's more than enough, Griffin thought.

"Where will I be staying?" Griffin asked.

"Glad you asked. You will be staying in the legendary Waldorf Astoria, just down the street. Are you familiar with the hotel?" Turnbull replied.

"I've heard of it," Griffin replied.

Again, everyone laughed so hard that they could be heard outside of the meeting room.

"Griffin, your innocence and youth are killing me," Mr. Turnbull said.

"Killing you?" Griffin asked.

"Yes, I love your enthusiasm, your innocence, and everything about you. I'd give anything to be that age again," Turnbull said.

He really is a cool dude, Griffin thought.

"Thank you, Mr. Turnbull," Griffin said.

Everyone stood from the boardroom table as Griffin stood to leave.

"So, we've got a deal, Griffin?" Mr. Turnbull asked as he reached out to shake Griffin's hand.

"Yes, we've got a deal," Griffin said as he shook Mr. Turnbull's hand and smiled.

"Thank you for your meeting today. We've got a winning author with a winning team. Here's to Griffin Smith and *A Novel Life*," Mr. Turnbull said as he lifted his glass from the table to toast in Griffin's honor.

"Thank you, Mr. Turnbull and staff. It was an honor meeting you," Griffin said.

Before Turnbull showed Griffin the door, he said a few final words.

"Your limo is waiting for you," Turnbull said.

***

I remember the day I met Mr. Turnbull. He had charm and charisma. Everything he was offering seemed so amazing. At the time, I thought I had it made. I was going to get a hundred-grand advance. I was on top of the world. Little did I know Mr. Turnbull had ulterior motives, and there was something in his facial expression and body language that was unsettling. He didn't look eager or professional, he looked startled and amazed, as though he'd just solved a particularly difficult puzzle. It wasn't until later I found out the real reason Turnbull signed me.

CHAPTER NINE
THE REVELATION

"Kelsey, hold my calls for the rest of the day. I've got something urgent to tend to," Mr. Turnbull said to his receptionist.

"Yes sir," she replied.

Mr. Turnbull had to be sure his intuition was correct; this was no coincidence.

He opened his personal laptop and clicked the file of the new novel he had completed. Then Turnbull opened the envelope he had received from Griffin Smith that held the manuscript of *A Novel Life*.

A Novel Life was going to be Turnbull's big comeback novel. He was ecstatic about it. Turnbull hadn't had a *New York Times* bestselling novel in ten years. He so desperately wanted to get back on the top of the charts as an author. Turnbull could taste it.

Mr. Turnbull read each manuscript and compared the words. His eyes were startled with surprise.

My hunch was right; Griffin Smith is the same Griffin I wrote about in my book. I saw him with my own eyes. I shook his hand," Turnbull thought.

Mr. Turnbull continued to read and compare manuscripts.

But I've never met him until today. How could I have described everything about him perfectly? Turnbull thought.

Mr. Turnbull sat in silence, thinking about the ramifications of the whole thing and how eerie it all was.

Could I have created a living and breathing character in my own book? Turnbull thought.

Mr. Turnbull noticed everything was the same, word-for-word between the book he had written and the *A Novel Life* Griffin had written and submitted to Turnbull. The stories and timeline were too close for comfort There were too many similarities to be purely coincidental.

Griffin Smith lives 800 miles away. He never had access to my manuscript. How could this be? Is it possible I can control Griffin's every action and move by what I write on the page? Turnbull wondered.

Mr. Turnbull pondered the thought that his written words could possibly control every word and action of Griffin.

That's nonsense. Griffin is alive, Turnbull thought.

But there was one way to find out if it was true. Mr. Turnbull spent the rest of his day making some changes to his new book. Turnbull re-wrote some chapters with distinct events that happened to Griffin Smith. These events could not be mistakenly confused by coincidence. Mr. Turnbull could determine if the same events occurred in Griffin's real life as the events written about Griffin Smith.

Soon the truth would be revealed.

***

For those of you who have read up to this point and possibly found some of the chapters to be unclear, please allow me to clarify. I am Carlton Tucker, the author of *A Novel Life*. I go by the AKA name, Griffin Smith, who is the protagonist in the book, *A Novel Life,* that I am writing. Griffin and I are one in the same. It is too personal for me to write a journal about myself using my real name. *A Novel Life* is a story about me. When Mr. Turnbull signed a book deal with Griffin, he signed it with me, Carlton.

CHAPTER TEN
I LOVE NEW YORK

The driver handed Griffin's bag to the bellhop at the front door. But before Griffin could follow him, he stopped to take a photo on his phone of the magnificent, legendary hotel.

"Wait just a minute, sir. I want to take a picture," Griffin said.

Griffin stepped back a few feet so he could capture the ornate gold sign engraved on the stone building framed by two large American flags. He got a few photos of the large words on the building that said: THE WALDORF ASTORIA. Griffin wanted some photos to show his family and friends—to prove to them that this trip was real, not a dream.

"Okay, I'm ready, sir."

The bellhop led Griffin through the heavy, brass-covered glass doors into an extraordinarily different world inside. His eyes grew wide with amazement as he admired the beige-colored marble everywhere—walls, ceiling, and floors. Griffin's Converse-clad feet climbed a flight of marble stairs and stood on a large circle design. It was a remarkable work of art with inlaid marble in various shapes and sizes on the floor. Two tall narrow brass vases stood on the stairway posts directly behind him. A corridor of marble with marble posts, palm trees, and a stunning ebony grand piano appeared in sight to the left of Griffin. Sure, Griffin had grown up in a very large city, but he had never seen anything like this before. It looked luxurious and very expensive, like a museum filled with valuable art.

Griffin didn't have a lot of money growing up. His parents struggled to pay the rent, groceries, and the basic things in life. Griffin wasn't used to luxury. His parents could barely afford to keep the lights on in their home.

Griffin continued to follow the bellhop toward an ornate, gold-decorated tall clock which resembled something you'd see in London. He turned left and stepped up to the fancy, solid-wood hotel counters where a friendly gentleman greeted him with a smile.

"May I help you?" the hotel clerk asked.

"Yes, I'm Griffin Smith. I'm staying for three nights, courtesy of Sheldon House Publishers."

"Oh, I see. How nice. Are you an author?" the clerk asked.

Griffin paused for a second to check his phone as it was vibrating in his pocket. Then he replied.

"Yes, I am signing a contract. I'm their youngest author ever," Griffin replied.

"Sweet. I'm Charles and I'll be helping you get checked in. Your ID please," the clerk said.

Griffin fumbled around searching through his pockets and then answered.

"Oh, yes, here's my driver's license," Griffin said.

The clerk looked at it and smiled.

"You're from Chicago?" Charles asked.

"Yes," Griffin answered.

"Well, welcome to New York," Charles said.

Griffin smiled from cheek to cheek and held his shoulders up proudly.

"Thank you," Griffin replied.

"Just sign here, and we'll get you to your suite right away," Charles said.

"Excuse me, but did you say suite?" Griffin asked.

Griffin's eyes grew wide with excitement. He had only dreamed of staying in hotel suites before. The best he could ever afford was a Super 8.

"Yes, I did indeed say suite You'll be staying in the Towers Luxury Guestroom Suite on the 42nd floor. It is exquisite," Charles replied.

"Wow, that's amazing," Griffin said.

"It's first-class luxury. You'll have everything—a sauna, bathrobe, twenty-four-hour room service, and cookies personally delivered to you before bed," Charles explained.

Just the thought of living in that much luxury all at one time sent shivers up Griffin's arms and legs.

Wow, Griffin, you've really arrived, staying in a luxury suite in New York City, he thought.

Griffin smiled at Charles as he signed the paperwork. The bellhop led him to the elevator. He pushed the up arrow. The solid brass elevator opened, and they stepped in. There wasn't anyone else on the elevator. The bellhop pushed number forty-two for Griffin's floor.

"I couldn't help but hear you say you're an author. What kind of books do you write?" the bellhop asked.

"This is my first novel. It is new adult," Griffin replied.

"Oh, a book for young adults?" the bellhop asked.

Griffin thought about how to answer his question. Then he replied.

"Sort of. The librarian back home says that they are the bestselling books. People ages seventeen to thirty years of age mostly read them," Griffin explained.

"Yeah, I heard those books have the best chances of becoming movies, too," the bellhop said.

"Really? Movies?" Griffin asked.

Griffin scratched his head at the thought of his book becoming a movie.

"Oh, yeah, many are turned into blockbuster movies like the *Hunger Games*. Perhaps your novel will become a major movie hit one day," the bellhop said.

"How do you know so much about all of this?" Griffin asked.

"I do a little writing myself. I haven't had anything published yet. But maybe one day I will," the bellhop said.

Before either of them could say another word, the elevator door opened to the 42nd floor—more of the same ornate marble and gold décor. The bellhop led Griffin down the long hall to room 4208.

"Here it is, your suite," the bellhop said.

"Thanks, dude. Here's a tip," Griffin said as he handed him a twenty-dollar bill.

God, that felt good to tip him a twenty, Griffin thought to himself.

Griffin felt like a different person. He had been struggling as a poor kid back in his hometown, and now he was handing the bellhop a twenty-dollar tip. Griffin's world had suddenly turned upside down. He felt like a young, successful millionaire who could flaunt what he had anytime he wanted to.

Is this the beginning of what my future life will be like? Griffin thought.

Griffin opened the ornate heavy-wooden door and stepped into paradise.

"If you need anything, don't hesitate to call room service," the bellhop said as he wished Griffin good luck.

"Okay, I will. Thanks for everything," Griffin replied. As Griffin stepped into his luxury suite, he couldn't believe all his eyes were taking in: high ceilings with crown molding, beautiful framed prints of contemporary artwork, long ritzy, colorful striped drapes in each window, a separate living room area, a marble bathroom with a sauna, a giant flat-screen television, and a wet bar. The view of the New York skyline from the 42nd floor was spectacular.

So, this is how the rich live, Griffin thought.

Griffin threw himself down on the plush, king-sized bed. It felt amazingly comfortable. It felt like the mattress, comforter, and pillows were all filled with goose feathers. He could have fallen asleep in the afternoon because the bed felt like paradise. But Griffin decided to leave his room and explore Manhattan. He found a safe in the closet of the room. Griffin called the front desk to get directions on how to set the combination. As soon as he set the combination, he decided to stash all but $500 in the safe. Griffin was not about to walk around the streets of New York with a $1,000 in his pocket. He wasn't about to get robbed.

Griffin grabbed his phone and closed the hotel door behind him. He took the hallway to the elevator, which took him to the lobby area, and he followed the marbled hallway down the stairs and out the large, brass front doors. It was only 4:30 p.m. Griffin had the rest of the night. He was in New York City, the center of the universe. He had a whole lot of celebrating to do before he flew out on Monday morning. It was party time. Griffin wandered down Park Avenue knowing it was going to be the best time of his life.

***

I can't believe how green and naïve I was at the time. I was so caught up in the rich and famous lifestyle at the moment that I couldn't see trouble waiting for me around the corner. It's funny, when you've been deprived of all that stuff for so long, and you suddenly stumble onto it, you can't get enough of it. That was me at the time—living in the lap of luxury.

CHAPTER ELEVEN
PARTY'S OVER, BACK TO THE GRIND

"Damn phone," Griffin shouted.

The hotel room phone rang too many times before Griffin answered it. He wanted to stay under his comfortable covers all day. But the obnoxiously loud phone ring wouldn't let him. Griffin threw his covers on the floor and forced his tired body to pick up the phone beside his bed.

"Yes?" Griffin said.

"This is your wakeup call from the front desk reminding you that you have a 10:05 a.m. flight this morning at LaGuardia," the voice said.

"What time is it?" Griffin asked.

Griffin was in a tug-of-war with his body. Part of him wanted to go back to sleep. The other half insisted he wake up.

"It's seven a.m.," the voice replied.

"Seven a.m.? It's too early," Griffin said.

"The staff at Sheldon House want to make sure you don't miss your plane," the voice said.

Griffin mumbled a few profanities under his breath. He spoke sarcastically. "Well, that's mighty kind of them," Griffin said in a flippant voice.

Griffin hung up the phone and headed for the shower. He threw his jeans, shirt, socks, and shoes on as quickly as he could. He threw his dirty laundry inside his bag. It was a sad day. Griffin had to leave this paradise for the grind again. He took a moment to appreciate life. He stopped for a long stare, taking in the panoramic view of his luxurious room for one last time. Griffin took one last long view of the city skyline from his window.

How can I ever live my ho-hum, boring life again after living in this paradise? Griffin thought to himself.

Griffin shrugged his shoulders and tried to pick himself up.

"It is what it is," Griffin told himself.

He pulled himself together and closed the hotel room door behind him. He took the long hallway to the elevator one last time. As the elevator door opened, Griffin bid the 42nd floor goodbye. He made his final round of the ornate gold and marble lobby as he descended the flight of stairs to the brass and glass doors of the Waldorf.

The long black limo was waiting for him.

Griffin stood in front of the hotel. The driver helped him into the car. He drove Griffin to the terminal of LaGuardia and helped him with his bag to the check-in counter. Griffin got his boarding pass and went through security with a breeze. When they called for him to board, Griffin walked slowly up the ramp to the plane and took his seat by the window in row 11A.

As his plane lifted off the runaway, Griffin bid New York City one last goodbye. He took one final view of the skyline as the plane lifted higher and higher toward the clouds. Griffin was sad. His life was so different in New York versus Chicago. But then the thought of his upcoming book tour lifted his spirits. Come September 15 next year, Griffin would no longer be living in Chicago. He would be traveling from city-to-city and across the United States meeting new faces and experiencing exciting places. Griffin would be taking in new sights, foods, and places to party. It was an unexplored world, and he would be living it up in less than a year.

New York was an amazing adventure. During Griffin's weekend, he saw so many new faces, took the subway to the Freedom Tower and Rockefeller Center, and ate a lot of pizza, bagels, and sushi. He had to admit, the millions of bright, colored lights in Times Square at night topped everything. They were more than his eyes could take in at once. It was a fun-packed weekend and Griffin hardly got any sleep. He'd be back in his hometown in less than three hours, and he would have to face another ho-hum day in Chicago.

CHAPTER TWELVE
ONLY 332 DAYS TO GO

Griffin couldn't wait to share the news with his parents.

His parents gave him a big hug and a smile when he walked through the front door. Griffin made it back safely from New York. And it just happened that his father was off on Mondays, so he could see Griffin too.

"How was New York?" Griffin's dad asked.

Wow is he in a good mood today. Maybe he really misses me. Perhaps he won't hit me, Griffin thought to himself.

"It was incredible. I got a contract offer on my new book and a $100,000 advance," Griffin replied.

"We are so proud of you, Son," Griffin's dad said.

"When do you get the $100,000?" Griffin's mom asked.

Griffin paused for a second to think about how to reply to his mom's question.

"As soon as I meet with a lawyer and get the contract approved," Griffin answered.

"Awesome, Son. We are proud of you," his mom said.

"Thank you. Mom, Dad, do you know any good entertainment or copyright lawyers?"

They stopped for a minute. There was a long pause of silence.

"Yes, I know someone who could help you. He could give you a cut-rate and maybe even do us a favor by not charging at all. He owes me a favor," Griffin's dad said.

"Awesome. Could you call him for me? I need to get this contract looked at ASAP." Griffin asked.

"Yes, Son, I will call him right now," his dad replied.

Wow, for once my dad is being nice and behaving himself, Griffin thought.

Griffin's dad stepped into the kitchen to make the call, so as not to interrupt Griffin's conversation with his mom about New York.

How considerate. Wonder how long this will last? Griffin thought.

"What was New York like?" his mom asked.

"It was paradise. The Waldorf suite was amazing," Griffin replied.

"Wait a minute, did you say you stayed in a suite in the Waldorf? his mom asked.

Don't get so excited, Mom, Griffin thought.

Griffin's mom had a beaming, giddy smile, like the face of someone who had won the lottery.

"Yes, you heard me right. I was treated like a king. I stayed on the 42nd floor in the Towers Luxury Guest Suites," Griffin said.

"That must have been amazing." his mom said.

"Now I know what it's like to be rich," Griffin replied.

Griffin's mom became quiet and still. She scratched her head with a puzzled look on her face. She was in a pensive mood. Then she spoke.

"Well, what was it like?" Griffin's mom asked.

"I had 24/7 room service, a marble bathroom with a sauna, and expensive meals delivered to my door. It was like living in a palace, and I was the king."

"Don't get too used to that. This is life after New York," his mom said.

Yeah, I know Mom. I get it, Griffin thought.

"Mom, I don't think I'll be living here for a very long time. I'll be out on the road for a year living in hotels. And who knows where I'll be living when I finally get back to Chicago," Griffin said.

Griffin's dad suddenly walked into the living room.

"I didn't mean to interrupt you, but you've got a meeting set for Friday at two p.m. He said he wouldn't charge you anything to look over the contract," Griffin's dad said.

"Thanks, Dad." Griffin said.

"Anything for you, Son," his dad replied.

Griffin pondered what his dad had just said.

What's with my dad? I leave for a few days and he changes into someone I don't even know.

"What's his name?" Griffin asked.

"Thurman Spielman," his dad replied.

What kinda name is that? Griffin thought.

"What's his address?" Griffin asked.

"He is in Willis Tower, 233 S. Wacker Drive, 58th floor," his dad said.

Griffin entered the address in his contact information on his phone.

"What's his number?" Griffin asked.

"It's 312-298-0098," his dad said.

Griffin entered the lawyer's number into his phone.

"Got it, Dad. Thanks," Griffin said.

For once, Griffin's dad flashed a warm smile at Griffin. It was a genuine smile. Griffin didn't want to call attention to his warm affection, so he started a little small talk

"Lucky, I only work at Home Depot until 11 a.m. this Friday," Griffin said.

"Well, hope you get the contract all straightened out," his dad said.

"Son, you'll do just fine," my mom said.

Griffin paused for a few seconds, not knowing how to continue the conversation.

"I hear you will be traveling a lot on your book tour," Griffin's dad added.

A little small talk too? Griffin thought.

"Yes, Mr. Turnbull's got me set for a sixty-city book tour of the U.S.," Griffin said.

"Wow, that's intense," his dad responded.

For some strange reason, the conversation started out lively and fast paced. Now it crawled along as if everyone had run out of what to say.

"Worse part is we won't get to see you for a long time," Griffin's mom said.

Maybe that's a good thing. Griffin thought.

"Oh, Mom, I'll still call you, and hopefully get to visit occasionally," Griffin said.

"Yeah, but it won't be the same as it is now," she replied.

Griffin reflected in silence on his mom's words.

"Mom and Dad, I love you dearly, but I'll be nineteen soon, and I need to live my dreams, too. That doesn't mean I won't miss you. You'll always be my mom and dad," Griffin said.

Not sure I'll miss you as much, Dad, Griffin thought.

Griffin's mom moved toward him and gave him a great big hug.

"You're right, Son. You are an adult now. We love you too, but we need to let you live your life and we need to be living ours," Griffin's mom said.

"Thanks, Mom."

"She's right, Son. As much as we love you, we still need to let you be your own person and let you grow up. We are so proud of you and the accomplishment of writing a bestselling novel," Griffin's dad said.

Did he really mean it? Is he proud of me? Could he really love me?

"Thanks, Dad."

Is this my new dad or is he putting on a front? Maybe he's changed because he knows one day soon, I'll be famous, Griffin thought.

"Well, I've got some catching up to do, so I'll talk to you later," Griffin said as he climbed the stairs to his room.

Whatever's going on with my dad, I like it. He isn't showing his anger, and he didn't try to hit me. But don't fool yourself, Griffin, he could strike like a cobra at any time, Griffin thought.

It was only 332 days and counting before Griffin's big tour. He was so ready.

CHAPTER THIRTEEN
WHAT WOULD A LAWYER DO?

Friday couldn't have come any sooner than it did. When Griffin got back from New York, he had to catch up on a lot of stuff and work extra hours at Home Depot due to the time he took off the previous week.

God, how long do I have to keep working here? I want to be on the road with my book tour, Griffin thought.

***

Once Griffin parked his car at the Willis Tower parking lot, he watched cars flying in both directions. Griffin rushed across the street to Willis Tower. It was a magnificent sight to see while standing next to it—up close and personal. He felt insignificant as he looked straight up at the never-ending stories that towered to the sky. It was one of the tallest buildings in the world with 110 stories, and Griffin was about to step inside.

Griffin took a few steps and entered the large glass doors that led to the lobby. The ceiling was extraordinarily tall with what seemed like hundreds of contemporary bright lights shining down. Columns of marble stood to the right and left. Griffin could see the first three floors of offices with nothing but glass framed by the columns. He stood in awe. He stepped up to the long dark, solid-stone counter located at the center of the first-floor lobby. Security was carefully watching everyone who entered the building. Griffin approached the receptionist seated at the counter.

"May I help you?" he asked.

"Yes, I have an appointment with Mr. Thurman Spielman on the 58th floor," Griffin replied.

"Your name?" he asked.

"Griffin Smith."

Griffin waited patiently while the receptionist called to confirm his two p.m. appointment.

"Mr. Spielman is expecting you. The office is Thomas, Gurstein and Spielman. They are on the 58th floor. Take the first elevator to the right. They are the first office on the floor," the receptionist said.

Griffin walked perhaps fifty feet around the corner and stood in front of the tall elevators. He pushed the up arrow and almost immediately the doors opened. The elevator was crowded with men and women dressed in suits and ties, but he managed to push the 58th floor button. A wide flat-screen TV inside the elevator welcomed visitors to the Willis Tower. A guide on the TV rattled off facts about the Willis Tower being the eighth tallest building in the world and that it took less than thirty seconds for the elevator to reach the 58th floor.

It's a good thing I'm not afraid of heights, Griffin thought.

The doors opened, and as Griffin stepped off the elevator, there it was—the office of Thomas, Gurstein and Spielman. The office was surrounded by glass with the large, eloquent silver logo piercing through the glass.

Griffin entered through large doors and an attractive red-haired receptionist flashed a big smile.

"How may I help you?" she asked.

"I have a two p.m. appointment with Mr. Spielman," Griffin replied.

"Your name please?" she asked.

"Griffin Smith."

As Griffin waited for her to call Mr. Spielman, he checked the time. His phone said it was 1:56 p.m. Perfect. he was on time and ready to get to his contract.

"Mr. Spielman is expecting you. He is running a little behind. Have a seat over there," the receptionist said as she pointed to the long wooden benches over in the corner.

"Thanks," Griffin said.

I sure hope he can help me. I hope I'm not wasting my time, Griffin thought.

Griffin sat patiently waiting for Mr. Spielman. He checked his text messages and surfed the web.

Griffin looked up and suddenly a medium-height, portly-looking man with short dark hair and a moustache approached him.

"You must be Griffin Smith," he said with a smile.

"I am Griffin."

He was friendly and reached out to shake Griffin's hand.

"Follow me to my office," he said.

Mr. Spielman carried a cane and walked with a limp on his left foot. He took his time getting to the office.

He shut the door behind him and sat comfortably behind his cluttered desk. It was difficult to really see because of all the piles of paper that covered his desk. Tall stacks of paper, books, and materials were piled on the floor to the left and right of him, randomly scattered everywhere.

What a messy lawyer. Does he ever throw anything away? Griffin thought.

"I'm glad you're here, Griffin," he said.

"Thank you," Griffin replied.

"Your dad has told me so many good things about you," Mr. Spielman said.

"Like what?" Griffin asked.

Griffin was anxious to hear what his dad had said about him. Mr. Spielman replied. "He is so proud of you getting your major book deal and your sixty-city tour."

My dad, proud of me. When did he ever show it until now? Griffin thought.

Memories Griffin remembered about his father were painful. Griffin tried to block those terrible scenes from his brain. Pictures of his father shoving Griffin against the closet door when he was six years old, and his father slamming his fists against Griffin's face. His bruises would always show the next day, and his mother would never

68

say anything for fear of being abused by Griffin's father. His mother would keep Griffin home for a week after he was beaten and bruised and claim to the school that he was sick.

"Your dad and I go way back. We've been friends for a long time," Spielman said.

My dad and him friends. I could never see that. They look like the unlikely kind to be friends. Besides, who would want to be friends with a monster? Griffin thought.

"Cool," Griffin said.

"I've been looking over your contract. Your dad faxed me a copy on Tuesday," Spielman said.

"Thank you for taking your time to check it out," Griffin replied.

"You're most welcome. Here's the bottom line. This contract seems too good to be true," Spielman said.

"What do you mean too good to be true?" Griffin asked.

So, Turnbull is going to screw me, Griffin thought.

"Just what I said, it's too good to be true—I can't find much fault with it. That's most unusual because usually, I make a lot of changes and negotiations with those big, powerful companies," Spielman said.

"Are you saying that Sheldon House is honest?" Griffin asked.

"No, I'm not making a judgement either way on whether they are honest or not," Spielman replied.

Griffin stopped in silence to think about what Spielman said.

"It's just that a lot of these big publishers get greedy and want to control everything. Mr. Turnbull could be a shady character," Spielman said.

Griffin thought some more about what Spielman said.

"I'll go through the contract with you and spell it all out in lay terms so you can understand," Spielman said.

"First, it's true you are giving up all of your rights to print your book worldwide. Most new authors give up their rights. That's not so bad because of all they are offering in return," Spielman continued.

What do you mean not so bad? I want to be treated fairly, Griffin thought.

"Like what?" Griffin asked.

"Sheldon House is giving you an advance of $100,000. That doesn't happen in today's publishing business. You are lucky if you get $10,000 tops. They must see you as a gold mine," Spielman said.

"Well, they said they had some big plans for me, whatever that means," Griffin replied.

"Keep in mind your $100,000 is an advance, not free money. If you sell 10,000 books at $25.95, you will be paid fifteen percent of the wholesale cost of the book, roughly $1.95 per book," Spielman said.

"I don't understand. Fifteen percent of the wholesale? Mr. Turnbull said I'd get paid ten percent," Griffin interrupted.

"Maybe he meant ten percent of the retail. This contract clearly states you get fifteen percent of the wholesale. If Mr. Turnbull is truly giving you ten percent of the retail you are getting more, $2.59 per book. But if he is giving you ten percent of the wholesale, you are making less at $1.29 a book," Spielman said.

Griffin's face looked confused and puzzled as he stopped to think about what Spielman said about the percentage of royalties due him.

"Perhaps you should call Mr. Turnbull and clarify the royalty rate before you sign this contract," Mr. Spielman said.

Griffin was growing weary of the royalty-talk rates. He stopped and listened without saying a word.

"Mr. Turnbull was partly correct. But in this contract, you have something better than ten percent. There is a sliding scale per the number of sales of your book. You start out with ten percent royalties for the first 9,999 copies sold. Then when and if you reach the 10,000 mark, you are paid fifteen percent. Should you be so lucky as to sell 100,000 or more copies, the rate goes to twenty percent," Spielman said.

"I hope I'm lucky enough to sell that many copies. I know there are no guarantees," Griffin said.

For a few seconds, Griffin thought about how sad it would be if he didn't sell many copies of his first book and if the book tour was a flop.

"That is different than Mr. Turnbull portrayed," Griffin said.

"Quite different, but a pleasant surprise working in your favor. So, as I was saying earlier, if you sell 10,000 copies as most books do for first-time authors, then your earnings would be about $19,500. There's only one problem with this," Spielman said.

10,000 copies, God, I hope I sell more than that, Griffin thought.

"What's that?" Griffin asked.

"Sheldon House would be taking a loss on you since they would be giving you $100,000 against the $19,500 you would earn, meaning you wouldn't see any more royalties until you made up the difference of $100,000 minus $19,500—a nice tax write-off for them," Spielman said.

"If that happened, it would be a disaster," Griffin said.

"You're telling me," Spielman replied.

"Okay, I understand all of that, but Mr. Turnbull says my book is going to be a *New York Times* bestseller and will sell millions of copies," Griffin said.

All at once, Mr. Spielman started laughing at the naivety of Griffin's comment.

"Son, I've got news for you. People in this business say a lot of things they don't really mean. Talk is cheap. It's all a bunch of hype. Mr. Turnbull is telling you what you want to hear. That's why you got people like me to shoot straight with you," Mr. Spielman said.

"Turnbull's probably going to screw me over like everyone else in my life has," Griffin mumbled under his breath.

"I don't mean to squash your dreams, Griffin. It's fun to dream and hopefully you will sell more than 10,000 copies. But you must be real. You must cut through all the hype and bull that these companies tell you. They'll try to paint the prettiest picture in the world, stoke your ego, and get you all fired up just so they can have control of your manuscript. Still, they must see some potential in you to offer you a $100,000 advance and to pay all your expenses to promote your book on a sixty-city U.S. tour," Spielman said.

"What kind of money are we talking about them spending to promote me for the tour?" Griffin asked.

"We are talking about at least $300 to $400 a day for your expenses, thousands of dollars in advertising, on top of the money they spent on courting you when you traveled to New York," Spielman said.

"Well how much are we talking about?" Griffin asked.

"It's hard to say, but if I had to guess I'd say a budget of $30,000 for your traveling expenses for the sixty-city tour, maybe an advertising budget of $60,000 and whatever they spent on you while you were in New York.," Spielman said.

Does this lawyer know what he's talking about? Griffin thought.

"Wow, that's a lot of money," Griffin said.

"Yea, I'd say they would pretty much own you with a spending budget of over $90,000 plus your $100,000 advance," Spielman said.

"That's kind of scary," Griffin said.

"Yes, it is, particularly if your books only sell 10,000 copies or less. They could stand to lose over $170,000. As you know, publishers don't like to lose money unless they need a big tax write off," Spielman said.

"That would be horrible if I caused Sheldon House to lose $170,000. I would be so embarrassed; I would never show my face around the hood again," Griffin replied.

"On the upside, if you got lucky and sold one million or more copies, you would have hit the jackpot. It would be like winning the lottery—possible, but rare," Spielman said.

I'm going to give it my all to promote my book, Griffin thought.

"Well, how much would I make if I sold at least a million copies?" Griffin asked.

"At the 20% rate of the wholesale price of $13.00 it would bring you about $2.60 per book. That doesn't sound like a lot, but when you multiply it by one million, you get $2,600,000," Spielman replied.

"Wow, that's a hell of a lot of money," Griffin said.

"Yes, there's no harm in dreaming. It is possible but not probable. If you deduct about the $90,000 they would be spending on you, including the $100,000 advance, that would leave you with $2,410,000," Spielman said.

Wow, I'd have to sell a shitload of books, Griffin thought.

"That's a whole lot of money," Griffin said.

"But, don't get your hopes up just yet. By the time you've paid your state and federal income taxes including Social Security taxes, you would end up with a little more than one million dollars," Spielman said.

"Wow, one million dollars for my age isn't bad money," Griffin said.

"I repeat, there's no harm in dreaming, just don't take your dreams too seriously," Spielman said.

Why not? Griffin thought.

"Oh, there is one more thing I need to tell you about the contract," Spielman said.

"What's that?" Griffin asked.

"You sell out all of your film and TV rights," Mr. Spielman said.

"What does that mean?" Griffin asked.

"It means Sheldon House owns your film and TV rights and if someone wants to make a movie or a television show you could stand to lose a lot of money," Spielman warned.

"What can I do about that?" Griffin asked.

"Nothing," Spielman answered.

"What do you mean I can't do anything about it? "Griffin asked.

"Griffin, you are green. You have never had a book published before. It's hard to demand things if you don't have some clout," Mr. Spielman said.

Griffin thought about what Mr. Spielman said. He realized Mr. Spielman was right. Griffin was green.

"Everything else about the contract looks good. I can't find any fault with it. I would say go for it. Sign it. You're young, what do you have to lose?" Spielman said.

"How do I know I can trust Mr. Turnbull?" Griffin asked.

"You don't know, but overall, the contract looks good," Spielman answered.

Griffin was quiet for a moment. He thought about all Spielman had said. He thought about the advantages and pitfalls.

***

"So, what do you think I should do?" Griffin asked.
"Griffin, I advise you to sign it. What do you have to lose?"
"My life."

CHAPTER FOURTEEN
OVERNIGHTING THE CONTRACT

Griffin rushed home to tell his parents about his meeting with Mr. Spielman. It was a wonder he didn't get stopped for speeding. Adrenaline rushed through Griffin's veins at lightning speed. He parked on the street in front of his house, walked through the iron gate, and climbed the steps to his front door. As he opened the door, Griffin greeted his mom with a great big smile and hug.

"How did your meeting go, Sweetheart?" Griffin's mom asked.

"It couldn't have gone any better. Mr. Spielman is a nice guy. Sometimes he's a little too pessimistic for me to handle. But he's for real. Best part of it all is that he didn't charge me for the visit. Says he owed Dad a big favor," Griffin said.

"That's terrific. I'm so proud of you. So, what did he say about the contract?" Griffin's mom asked.

"He said he looked it over and couldn't find fault with it. He said it was too good to be true," Griffin replied.

"Wonderful. Sounds like you've got a really good company with Sheldon House," Griffin's mom said.

"I hope so. They seem very supportive. They seem to believe in me," Griffin replied.

"What are your plans?" his mom asked.

"I'm going to sign this contract while I'm still stoked. I'm going to rush down to the post office and overnight it to Mr. Turnbull," Griffin said.

"That's wonderful, Griffin. Go for your dream, your dad and I are one hundred percent behind you," his mom said.

Griffin's mom threw her arms around Griffin and gave him a big kiss.

"Oh, Mom, I'm a grown man," Griffin said as he blushed.

She hugged him again and gave him another kiss.

"Oh, okay, a grown man can still love his mom, can't he? I do love you, Mom. Thanks for always believing in me," Griffin said.

"You are so welcome," she replied. There was a pause of silence. Then she smiled.

"Go on and get your contract mailed. Don't let me keep you," she said as she patted Griffin on the back.

Griffin returned the smile, blew her a kiss, and closed the front door behind him. He walked the front steps down to their black iron gate. The post office was only a couple blocks from his house. Griffin walked with his shoulders held high. He walked like he was somebody. He held the contract in a large manila envelope tucked under his arms. Griffin Smith was somebody. The world just didn't know it yet.

But after Griffin's first novel was released, the world might know his name—Griffin Smith.

As he entered the U.S. Post Office, Griffin noticed a long line. He walked over to the self-serve counter and wrote a short note on a piece of paper:

Dear Mr. Turnbull, I enjoyed meeting you in New York. I am excited to work with you on my new novel. Here's the signed contract. I'm ready to go.

Sincerely, Griffin Smith.

Griffin signed both copies of the contracts and addressed the envelope. The clerk noticed his writing on the front of the envelope.

"Are you an author?" she asked.

"Why, yes, first time," Griffin replied.

"How exciting," she said as she smiled at him.

"My very first contract is in there," Griffin said proudly.

"Wow, that's impressive with such a large book publisher. How old are you?" the clerk asked.

"Eighteen," Griffin replied.

"Wow, that's even more impressive. Good luck with your writing. That will be $22.95. It is guaranteed to get to New York tomorrow by noon," the clerk said.

"Thank you." Griffin said as he handed her the money.

"You are welcome. Good luck with your contract and book deal. I look forward to seeing your book in the stores," the clerk said.

"Me too. It's called *A Novel Life* and it will be in all bookstores everywhere by September 15 of next year," Griffin said.

"Awesome," she said.

"Oh, by the way, I'm Griffin Smith. Don't forget my name."

CHAPTER FIFTEEN
WAITING ON ONE HUNDRED GRAND

Where's my one hundred-grand? Griffin asked himself.

The weekend passed and Griffin didn't hear anything from Sheldon House. Of course, he had overnighted his contract to Mr. Turnbull on a Friday expecting it to get there the next day. And it probably would have arrived Saturday, but no publishing company in New York would be open on a Saturday. Griffin figured that Mr. Turnbull would open his package with his signed contract Monday. He was anxious about receiving his check for $100,000. Griffin had never seen that much money in his whole life. The week passed as he ran to the mailbox every day after work. Griffin quizzed his mom and dad each day to see if they had seen an important letter or package addressed to him. It was killing him to wait for that check.

Each day was the same ho-hum drudgery. Griffin would get up early, go to work at Home Depot, and come home to find no check waiting for him. The week passed and still no check. Griffin was growing frustrated. Still no check. Was Mr. Turnbull not interested in him anymore? Did Turnbull lie to him?

Griffin felt like a giant vacuum cleaner had sucked the soul out of him. He was ready to give up all hope of ever receiving that check for one-hundred-grand. One day Griffin came home from work tired and feeling defeated.

"Sweetheart, I have something special for you today," Griffin's mom said.

"You might want to look at this express mail envelope. It came today, and I had to sign for it. I think this might brighten your spirits," his mom said.

"Did you say envelope as in possibly a check for one-hundred-grand?" Griffin asked.

"Here it is. Open it," his mom said.

Griffin tore open the envelope and left it in pieces on the floor. He couldn't believe his own eyes as he examined what he held in his hands—a check for $100,000. The check was made out to Griffin Smith. It was a cashier's check, which meant it wouldn't be held by his bank. He could use it for whatever he wanted to—right now. Griffin lit up.

"Look, Mom. Can you believe this? It's true what they told me. I'm actually holding $100,000 in my hands," Griffin said.

"That's unbelievable, Griffin," his mom said.

She reached over, wrapped her arms around Griffin with all her might, and gave him a kiss. She was jumping up and down, doing the happy dance all around the living room.

"It's time for us to celebrate, Griffin," she said.

Griffin's mom couldn't contain her excitement. She was acting as though she had just received a check for $100,000 herself.

"Wait till your dad gets home. I can't wait for you to show him."

"Are you kidding? Hold on to this check until Dad gets home?" Griffin asked.

"I'd thought you would show him," his mom said.

"I can't wait to get this check to the bank. I'm not going to show it to Dad," Griffin said.

"Well, okay, then at least let me take some pictures of you holding the check. You can show your dad when he gets home," she said.

Griffin's mom reached for her phone and held it up.

"Smile, Griffin; you've just received a $100,000 check. Hold it up proudly," she said as she took some photos.

"That's all you get, Mom. I love you, but I am going to the bank and depositing this check," Griffin said.

Griffin grabbed a soda pop from the kitchen and ran toward the door.

"What are you going to do with the money?" Griffin's mom asked.

"I haven't decided yet. I've got some ideas though," Griffin replied.

"Before you go, I'd like to tell you again how proud your dad and I are of you," his mom said.

"I know, Mom, you've told me a thousand times," Griffin said.

"Well that's because I really mean it," Griffin's mom said.

"Bye, Mom. I'm going to the bank," Griffin said as he opened the front door.

"Be careful. You're carrying a lot of money on you. Listen, when you get back, I'm going to suggest that your dad and I take you to a wonderful restaurant to celebrate your success," Griffin's mom said.

"Okay, Mom. That's nice. I'll think about it. I'm going now, bye," Griffin said.

Griffin closed the front door behind him, walked down the concrete steps and sidewalk, and closed the iron gate.

Griffin felt rich, and he was on his way to the bank.

***

The excitement and joy I felt that day when I received the hundred-grand check still feels as real today as it did back then. I had to put my laptop down after I finished this chapter and reflect with celebration and joy. And though money doesn't fix everything, it helped boost my damaged self-esteem. I felt important and like I could do anything. Growing up was rough and painful with an abusive father and being bullied by those who were taller and stronger than me. It didn't help my self-esteem growing up with a mother who seldom paid me any attention.

I had a chip on my shoulder—always angry. I have carried this anger around with me till this day.

CHAPTER SIXTEEN
WHAT TO DO WITH ONE HUNDRED GRAND

One hundred grand is burning holes in my hands like kryptonite, Griffin thought.

Griffin stood in line at Bender Bank with his $100,000 check in hand. He couldn't wait to see the reaction of one of the tellers when he handed her the check. There was one man ahead of Griffin. Soon he would be able to deposit his long-anticipated check. He had planned on depositing it into his savings account. He had a little money in his savings—perhaps $100 or $150. Griffin had opened that account in hopes of saving some money from his Home Depot job, but every time he tried to put some away, he'd have to use it to fix his car or pay for some unexpected expense. Griffin felt good that he finally had some real money to save.

It was Griffin's turn to step up to the teller window. He walked with his head held high, shoulders straight, and flashed a big, confident smile.

"May I help you?" the pretty brunette teller asked.

"I would like to make a deposit into my savings account," Griffin said.

"May I see your ID?" she asked.

"Here," he said.

Griffin handed her the check. He watched her eyes grow wide with amazement when she read the amount.

"How old are you?" she asked.

"Eighteen," Griffin answered.

"That's quite a bit of money you have here for someone your age," the teller said.

Griffin paused for a second to search for the words to say to the teller.

"Yeah, this is my advance for my new novel which is coming out next September," he said proudly.

"Congratulations," the teller said.

"Thank you," Griffin replied.

She turned the check over and handed it to him.

"Here, sign the back and put your account number below your signature," the teller said.

Griffin signed the back of the check, wrote his account number below his name, and handed it back to her.

"Are you wanting any money back today?" she asked.

"Yes, I'd like $9,000 please. I'm thinking about buying a Kawasaki bike," he replied.

"No problem. I can help you with that," the teller said as she smiled at him.

Griffin stood at the teller window and waited patiently. The teller counted the bills carefully.

His heart raced ahead. He took a few slow deep breaths and exhaled. Griffin had never held that much cash in his hands before.

The teller placed nice crisp bills underneath the teller window. Griffin scooped the bills up with both hands and meticulously placed them in his wallet in his back jeans pocket. She handed him a receipt with his printed balance and smiled at him.

"Congratulations again. Have a wonderful day. Oh, and good luck with spending that money," the teller said.

"Thank you," Griffin said. He returned the smile.

As Griffin walked through the bank door and out to the parking lot, he wasn't paying attention to where he was walking. His eyes were glued to the bank receipt which said he had $91,124.06 left. Griffin had to look at it again. It was hard to believe he had that much money in his bank account.

Griffin walked past a row of thick and tall shrubs planted in a remote parking area where his car was waiting for him. Before he could unlock his car, Griffin felt the cold, hard nozzle of a pistol being shoved up against the lower side of his back. He heard a deep voice warning him.

"Don't make any sudden moves and no one will get hurt," the voice commanded.

It happened so fast, it caught Griffin by surprise. He couldn't see who was holding the gun because his back was against the intruder's face. Then Griffin heard the hammer being pulled back. It made a dreadful sound. He froze in his tracks and trembled with fear. The slightest twitch of the invader's hand would put a large hole through Griffin's kidney and his upper intestines. He had no choice but to cooperate.

"Place your hands slowly on the car window. Slowly," the voice said.

Griffin reached both hands and touched them firmly against the glass. He could feel his wallet being lifted from his back pocket. Suddenly, Griffin was back at Wendell Fentress High. His mind flashed back to the horrific scene of himself being brutally beaten and hung up by his feet in the men's bathroom. The memory was so painful to see in his mind that the palm of his hands started sweating profusely. Griffin's hands slid down the glass of the car window. He couldn't hold his hands in one place.

"Aw, how much do we have here?" the voice asked.

Griffin didn't say a word and remained frozen.

The robber was silent while he counted the bills tucked inside Griffin's wallet.

"Well, what do you know, it's my lucky day, nine grand. I hit the jackpot," the voice said.

The robber laughed uncontrollably like the Joker did in *Batman*.

"Now move slowly and into your car. Easy, and don't turn around," the voice commanded.

Griffin did as the robber said. He turned his eyes and face away from the invader, opened his car door slowly, and lowered his body to sit in the driver's seat. The robber slammed Griffin's car door and in a split second he was gone. It was like his worst nightmare, only it was really happening. His body slumped in the driver's seat, eyes staring at the steering wheel, Griffin was suspended in a state of shock. The brutal scene of Griffin hanging upside down over the toilet in the men's bathroom at his old high school, followed by Griffin continually being whipped with a leather belt by his father when he was eight years old flashed back in Griffin's mind. As hard as Griffin tried to erase these disturbing images he couldn't. They haunted him repeatedly.

How could Griffin have been that foolish to carry so much cash with him? How could he have been stupid enough to allow himself to be robbed? What would he tell his parents?

Griffin felt crushed and violated. He felt like crying. That was his money, he had received for the book he had written. And in a few seconds, $9,000 was gone. Still, Griffin realized he could have been killed today, and life to him was more important than any amount of money.

His hands, arms and legs still shook from being caught by surprise with a gun nozzle pushed deep into his lower back. He sat in his car for the longest time, frozen and suspended in time.

Finally, Griffin decided what he would do. He called the police and painfully waited for them

CHAPTER SEVENTEEN
HOW TO TELL YOUR PARENTS YOU'VE BEEN ROBBED

Griffin opened the front door of his house slowly and tip-toed, one step at a time, toward his bedroom, hoping his mom wouldn't hear him come in. He had just finished talking to the police while they filled out a robbery report, and he was exhausted.

"Did you get your check deposited?" a voice said from a distance.

The voice was his mom. She was waiting for him to return from the bank. His mom was seated on the couch in the living room. Griffin pretended he didn't hear her and continued climbing the stairs. Before he could climb another step, he heard her voice speak again.

"Did you have any trouble depositing your check?" Griffin's mom spoke louder.

Griffin realized he was busted, and his mom wouldn't let it go. He turned around and walked down the stairs toward the living room. Griffin's shoulders were slumped, and he held his head down low. Griffin's mom noticed his whipped, puppy-dog demeanor.

"Are you alright, Griffin? You don't look so good," his mom asked.

Griffin stopped in his tracks and paused in silence for a moment.

"No, Mom, I'm not alright," Griffin said.

"Come over here and sit down beside me. Tell me what's going on," his mom said.

Griffin moved in closer to where his mom was sitting and sat beside her on the couch.

His mom acted as though she genuinely cared. She moved closer to Griffin and put her arms around him. So, what if his mom hadn't been there for him for eighteen years of his life; she was there for him now at one of his lowest moments, and that's all that counted. Griffin's mom waited in silence for Griffin to speak.

"I got robbed," Griffin mumbled under his breath.

"What?" his mom replied.

"I got robbed," Griffin confessed.

"Oh, Sweetheart, I am so sorry, did they take your check?"

"No, Mom, that is safe in the bank,"

"What did they take then?" his mom asked.

"I asked for $9,000 in cash back. Someone shoved a gun in my back when I came out of the bank," Griffin said.

Griffin's mom moved closer to Griffin and held him tighter.

"Oh dear, that is horrible," his mom said. Tears began to stream from her eyes.

"Yes, it was. They lifted my wallet and took nine-thousand dollars from me. I am sick over it," Griffin said.

"I know you must be sick. But thank God you are alive," his mom said.

His mom's face looked pained and distraught. She was weeping.

"Did you see the robber's face?" his mom asked.

"No, he held his gun behind me the whole time," Griffin replied.

"I am so sorry, Griffin," his mom said.

"Thank you, Mom. I told the police everything. They said they've had a string of robberies in that area in the last two months."

"I am thankful you are alive, Griffin," his mom said. Griffin's mom hugged him tighter. Then she reached toward him and kissed Griffin on the cheek.

"Thank you, Mom. I needed that."

"You're welcome, Son, anytime. It's in the hands of the police now," his mom said.

"Yep, and I doubt I'll ever see that money again," Griffin said.

"You might not, but think of it this way, you're alive, and before you signed that contract, you had no money," his mom said.

"True, Mom, very true," Griffin said.

"As hard as this day has been for you, Griffin, you must try your best not to let it ruin your days ahead."

"Before I was robbed, I dreamed about all the things I could buy. I thought about fast bright-red convertibles, the latest motorcycles, partying in Vegas, hanging with the hottest girls, and throwing some big parties," Griffin said.

"Don't stop dreaming, Griffin. You're alive and you still have over $90,000 in the bank," his mom said.

Sadly, Griffin didn't have any real friends. He wasn't popular like some of the others in school. Griffin was too into himself with his writing fixation and dreams. Jonah, Justin, and Ashlee were his acquaintances. They were nerdy too. They understood him and were into the same thing he was—writing. Many times, they were too busy to socialize. Griffin had money; maybe he'd start to get some friends.

They would see how cool he was with all the things money could buy and overlook the nerdy side of him. There were thousands of things he could do with the money. Griffin's mind raced through many of them. It was fun to dream but harder to know what to do with it. After all, Mr. Turnbull made it clear that the money was not free money, but an advance. Part of him wanted to be careful and cautious about how he spent it. But a loud voice in his head said, "Griffin, spend it while you have it, spend it now."

Griffin had been quiet for a while and hadn't said a word. His eyes were staring out into space.

"Penny for your thoughts, Griffin?"

"I was dreaming again about what to do with the money."

"Good, Son. I'm glad to see you dreaming again. I know it's killing you to lose that money, but you're alive. You're my son, and I am thankful for that," Griffin's mom said.

Thank you, Mom. Thank you for listening."

"You're welcome. It'll be okay, Son," his mom replied.

"But what do I tell Dad when he gets home?"

CHAPTER EIGHTEEN
THE CAR OF MY DREAMS

Griffin decided to put his recent robbery behind him, at least for now. His mind was filled up with $90,000, and he thought of all the ways he could spend it.

The week crawled slowly with the long hours working at Home Depot. Griffin couldn't wait until Saturday came. Usually, Saturday was one of the days he'd sleep in until noon. But Griffin couldn't sleep and woke up at seven a.m. He was so lit up that he jumped into the shower and quickly dressed into his jeans and a T-shirt. Griffin grabbed a pop tart and some juice.

"Bye, Mom and Dad. I'll be back sometime at the end of the day," Griffin said as he rushed out of the front door.

Griffin ran down the steps and through the gate to his car. He started it and headed to the I-294 Expressway entrance which took him to downtown. Griffin took the Cicero exit and finally reached his destination—Windy City Motors. As he pulled his car into the lot, his heart was pumping adrenaline through his body faster than a race car moving at top speed around the raceway. There it was, his dream car in his favorite color. Griffin's heart raced faster as he closed his car door behind him and stepped up to the car of his dreams—a new, bright green, GT-350 Mustang. Griffin had read that with its V8 super horsepower engine, it was possible to go from zero to sixty in about four seconds. That was one fast, mother of a car. Griffin spent a lot of time reading the reviews. The GT-350 was the car for him. No other car would do.

Griffin stood in front of his dream car and stared at her, admiring her beauty and contour.

If I only had a girlfriend. I'd cruise the town with her, Griffin thought.

Griffin's daydream was interrupted when a short, stocky middle-aged man approached him.

"She's a beauty, isn't she?" he asked.

"No kidding. That's one hot car," Griffin said. "I would love to take it out on the road."

Griffin stood in front of the car dreaming. He could see himself as a famous author driving around in that fast GT-350. Griffin imagined what people would say. They would think he was hot.

This is your car, Griffin. It's got your name written all over it, Griffin thought.

"I love this car," Griffin said.

"Is this a graduation gift from your parents?" the salesman asked.

"Are you kidding? My parents could never afford this car," Griffin replied.

"Well, do you have a rich uncle or some rich grandparents who will be buying this for you?" the salesman asked.

"No," Griffin answered.

"How old are you?" the salesman asked.

"Eighteen," Griffin replied.

"Well, do you have a job?" the salesman asked.

"Yeah, I work at Home Depot," Griffin replied.

The salesman broke out in a non-stop, uncontrollable, loud laughter which could be heard all over the parking lot. Griffin's jaw dropped, his shoulders and head fell in humiliation. Suddenly, his mind flashed back to his last day at William Fentress High when he was utterly humiliated by Rocky and Bull Dawg. Griffin could not erase that brutal, defeating last day.

"Son, I hate to break this to you, but do you know how much this car sells for?" the salesman said.

"No, not really," Griffin replied.

"This car loaded is $42,896 plus taxes, license and tags. Do you know how much the monthly payments are on this car?" the salesman said.

"No," Griffin replied.

"The payments are $647 a month, the salesman said.

"Seriously?" Griffin said.

"Yes, seriously. Cars cost a lot these days," the salesman said.

"You're right about that. Well, if I were to buy this car with cash, how much could I get it for?" Griffin asked.

"Cash, what kind of kid has that kind of money?" the salesman asked.

"I have over $90,000 in the bank," Griffin said proudly.

"And I own Disneyland," the salesman said.

The salesman continued to laugh uncontrollably. Griffin didn't laugh. His eyes stared at the salesman with disgust. Griffin didn't appreciate being ridiculed and made fun of in front of his face. Finally, the salesman stopped his laughter and held his tongue.

"You have ninety grand in the bank? Seriously?" the salesman asked.

"Yes, seriously. And if you don't want my business, I can go up the street to the Ford dealer there," Griffin said with a serious tone in his voice.

The salesman let out an even bigger laugh than before. Griffin waited for him to pause.

"What's so funny?" Griffin asked.

"Kid, what kind of joke are you playing on me? Do I look like a fool?" the salesman asked.

"No. But I'm not playing a joke on you. It's for real, I have over ninety grand in the bank," Griffin said.

"So, if I did believe you, how did you get ninety grand?" the salesman asked.

"I signed my first book deal with Sheldon House Publishers in New York, and they sent me a $100,000 advance. But I got robbed yesterday, so now I only have ninety-one grand." Griffin said.

"You got robbed, blah, blah, blah. And now you only have ninety-one grand," the salesman said in a mocking way. But he wasn't laughing anymore. He was piping mad.

"Kid stop lying to me. You're wasting my time. Get the hell out of here and don't come back," the salesman said.

Griffin had all he could take from the belligerent salesman. Griffin was done with him. He would find someone who would take him seriously.

***

I remember the time that salesman made me feel so small on the inside and out. The nerve of him to treat me the way he did. I was so disgusted; I gave up on the idea of the Mustang as my dream car. And I swore I would never do business with that dealership again.

CHAPTER NINETEEN
MY SECOND-BEST DREAM

Griffin jumped into his beat-up old car and headed down Cicero. His dream of buying a fast-new Mustang was thrown under a fast-moving train. Griffin was no longer in the mood to buy a car.

As Griffin drove down Cicero, he began to think about the money he had available and how much a new GT-350 Mustang would have cost him.

By the time Griffin paid $46,000 on a new Mustang with tax, tags, title, and insurance, he would really be looking at over fifty-grand. That was a whole lot of money to spend since Griffin still had plans to throw a book-launch party, save some, and pay taxes to the IRS. As much as he wanted that Mustang, Griffin felt uncomfortable about spending so much money on a car. Besides, it would be his advance he would be spending. He wouldn't even start to earn it back until late next year. The salesman who laughed in his face left a bad taste in his mouth about buying a Mustang.

Griffin's thoughts turned to his second-best dream: a brand-new Kawasaki KX250F street bike. It was a beauty, super-fast, and painted bright, neon green with gray coloring. It was hot. With the bike fresh on his mind, Griffin set his GPS to take him to Acme Cycle Shop located on West Belmont Avenue. Griffin followed the GPS and finally pulled into the Acme parking lot.

There it was, Griffin's dream bike. There were no other bikes like it. Griffin had thoroughly researched the KX-250F and he didn't care to look at any others. This was the one. He couldn't believe it. It was as if the bike had a sign on it that said, "Take me home."

Griffin jumped out of his car totally hyped. His heart raced as he took a few steps toward her and put his hands on the shiny, metallic handlebars. Griffin stared at her, dreaming of what it would be like cruising down the highway on that Kawasaki.

His daydream was cut short when a tall, muscular-built, tattooed man dressed in a black leather jacket and denims approached Griffin.

"She's smoking hot," he said.

"You're right; she's hot," Griffin replied.

"Would you like to take her out on the road?" the man asked.

"Yes, you bet," Griffin answered.

"Let me see your license, son," he demanded.

Griffin pulled the license out of his wallet from his back pocket and handed it to the salesperson.

The salesman examined Griffin's license closely.

"That's what I thought, this is a car driver's license. You need a motorcycle license to drive this."

"Oh, okay. That's good to know," Griffin said.

"But, no worries," he said as he handed Griffin back his license. "I'm Buck."

"I'm Griffin."

"Good to meet you," he said as he reached his hand out to shake Griffin's hand.

Buck placed a license on the back of the bike and handed Griffin a helmet. They put on their helmets.

"You can hop on the back, and I'll drive," he said. "That's as close as you can get to a driving experience right now until you get your motorcycle license. It's not hard to get. You take a written test and then drive your bike around a track for the driving test," Buck said.

"Thanks for the info," Griffin said.

Buck and Griffin both mounted the bike and then Buck fired it up. Griffin could hear and feel the power of the 249-cc engine as Buck revved it up.

"This has a five-speed transmission," Buck shouted over the engine noise. "Are you ready for the ride of your life?"

"You bet," Griffin shouted

Buck gunned the bike and turned left onto West Belmont Avenue. He was taking them to the Expressway. They merged onto the ramp, and next thing he knew, they were cruising at seventy miles per hour. They zoomed past cars at lightning speed. Griffin could feel the rush of the wind against his face and back. It was an amazing feeling, like no other feeling on this Earth. Griffin felt wild and free. He imagined what it would feel like to have a hot girlfriend with her arms tightly wrapped around his body, riding with him as her head was buried on his shoulder. It suddenly hit Griffin—this bike was for him, not the Mustang GT. From the moment, they put their helmets on to the moment Buck took them back to the parking lot, Griffin knew what he had to do—he had to buy that bike and get his motorcycle license as soon as possible.

Buck parked the bike, and they jumped off as he put the kickstand down.

"Well what do you think?" Buck asked.

"I'll take it," Griffin said.

"But you don't even know how much it costs," Buck said.

"I don't care how much it costs, I'll take it," Griffin said.

"But you don't know if you can afford it," Buck said.

"Oh, I can afford it, no problem," Griffin replied.

"Okay. The bike today, fully loaded with a twelve-month warranty, is $8,944. But with taxes, title, and registration the total comes to a grand total of $10,285. If you finance it over four years, the cost of the bike would be $14,295. You can get an extended warranty for $1,000 more," Buck said.

"No problem," Griffin replied.

This time there were no sudden outbursts of laughter. Buck took Griffin seriously. He didn't question Griffin about being too young, or where he worked, or how he was going to pay for it. Buck believed Griffin.

"The monthly payments on this bike are $300," Buck said.

"I'm not planning on making monthly payments," Griffin said.

Buck scratched his head. His faced looked puzzled. "How are you going to pay for it?" Buck asked.

"I'm paying cash," Griffin said

"Oh, okay, then. Cash it'll be," Buck said.

"I need to go to the bank and get it out of my savings," Griffin said.

"Wow, kid, are you rich?"

"You could say that," Griffin replied with a grin.

"If you are paying cash, the price is less because I was figuring in the cost of interest," Buck said.

"So, what is the cash price?" Griffin asked.

"Ten thousand two hundred and eighty-five dollars includes tax, tags, and a twelve-month warranty," Buck said.

That leaves me with about eighty-grand still left in my account to spend on other things, Griffin thought. "Could you hold this bike for me?" Griffin asked.

"Yes, but I can only hold it till five p.m. today," Buck replied

"Okay, terrific. The bank is open until one p.m. I'll be back," Griffin said

"See you soon, Griffin," Buck said.

Griffin hopped into his car, started it, and took a right turn on West Belmont Avenue. It was 11:30 a.m., and he was getting hungry, so he decided to make a drive-thru run at Wendy's for a number one with a large Coke and a chocolate frosty.

After Griffin's short visit at Wendy's, he continued to drive down West Belmont Avenue, searching for a Bender Bank branch. He looked to the left and right as Griffin chomped on his burger, washing it down with a Coke.

As Griffin drove, he asked Siri for help.

"Bender Bank on West Belmont Avenue," Griffin said.

"Bender Bank is located at 4824 West Belmont Avenue," Siri answered.

Griffin's GPS said he only had five more blocks to go. He was lit up again. The thought of withdrawing $10,285 for his new bike made him feel like he was on top of Mount Everest. It was a super rush that very few have ever felt.

Griffin reached his destination, parked his car in the back lot of the bank, and got out, shutting the door behind him. He ran to the bank door, opened it, entered the lobby, and picked up a withdrawal slip by the counter. Griffin carefully wrote his name, the date, account number, the amount, and signed it. He stood in line.

When it was his turn, Griffin stepped up to the counter and handed the withdrawal slip to the teller.

"Good morning," the teller said with a big smile.

"Morning," Griffin said with overwhelming confidence.

"ID please," the teller said.

Griffin reached into the back pocket of his jeans and pulled out his driver's license from his wallet.

"Here it is," Griffin said.

"Thank you," the teller said.

Griffin waited.

"Okay, here's how it works. Because of bank policy, I can't give you $10,285 in cash, but instead, I can give you a cashier's check, which is the same as cash. Is that acceptable?" the teller said.

"Yes, if that's the only way you can do it," Griffin said.

"Also, for your information, anytime one of our customers makes a deposit or withdrawal of $10,000 or more, we have to report it to the IRS But don't be alarmed, it's only so that the IRS knows you're not laundering money or conducting any illegal activities," the teller said.

"That's good to know," Griffin replied.

"Who do I make the check out to?" she asked.

"Acme Cycle Shop," Griffin said.

"Okay, thanks, I'll be right back," the teller said.

Griffin could hear her preparing his cashier's check for the bike. Griffin's mind flashed back to less than an hour earlier when Buck took him for a ride on his dream bike. It was a ride like no other. Griffin felt freedom with the wind against his face, cruising down the highway. There was hope for him yet in getting a girlfriend. Then his dream was interrupted.

"Here's your cashier's check. Please check to make sure all the information is correct. This is as good as cash, so don't lose it," the teller said.

Griffin's eyes scanned the check carefully.

"Looks good," he said.

"Then you're good to go," she said with a cheerful-looking smile.

Griffin looked over his shoulders for any would-be robbers, started the engine, and headed up West Belmont Avenue toward Acme Cycle Shop. The GPS said he had only fifteen blocks to go. The anticipation of waiting for his dream bike was killing him. Griffin couldn't stand it any longer. He pressed his foot on the gas pedal so he could get there sooner.

Finally, Griffin arrived back at Acme Cycle Shop. He turned into the parking lot, hopped out of his car, and rushed with sheer excitement toward the sales office.

"I've got the check, Buck," Griffin said.

"I was getting ready to leave for lunch. You caught me just in time," Buck said.

"Here's the check for the bike," Griffin said as he handed it to him.

Buck looked at it and had to take a second look just to make sure he was seeing it correctly.

"Yep, that's the right amount," he said.

"When can I get my bike?" Griffin asked.

"Slow down, boy, we've got some paperwork to do."

Griffin looked disappointed as his smile turned to a frown.

"Don't fret it. Everyone fills out the paperwork even if you're paying with cash. Besides, you still need to get your motorcycle license before you can drive it. That means we'll need to deliver it to your address," Buck said.

"Oh, I forgot about that," Griffin replied.

Griffin wouldn't be able to take his first ride of freedom until the end of the next week. He was bummed out, but it was what it was.

"Follow me to my office, and we'll get the paperwork done on your bike," Buck said.

Griffin followed Buck to his office and began the paperwork. Buck explained how the warranty worked and how Griffin needed to care for his bike. He handed Griffin temporary plates and the owner's manual. Griffin had to fill out the registration and title work for his Kawasaki. It only took an extra hour of his time.

"So, Buck, what is your best guess on how long it will take before I can take this baby on the road?" Griffin asked.

"Well, you've got to study for your test and practice somewhere with your bike. Your bike will be delivered on Monday or Tuesday. If you're a fast learner, and you get down to the DMV by Tuesday or Wednesday, you might be lucky enough to get your Kawasaki on the road by next weekend," Buck explained.

Griffin stopped for a moment and thought about what Buck had said. He took a deep breath and smiled.

"It will definitely be worth the wait."

***

When I bought my Kawasaki, I forgot all about ever wanting the Mustang. The bike was so me. I couldn't wait to cruise down the highway with the wind to my face, feeling the sweet taste of freedom.

CHAPTER TWENTY
DRESSING THE PART

Today was a happy day for Griffin because he got his motorcycle license. Griffin studied hard, practiced with his bike, and it all paid off for him.

If I'm going to show off my bike and find a hot girlfriend. I'll need to look like a biker, Griffin thought.

Griffin pulled out of the DMV building as fast as he could in his car. He was starving, so he made a quick drive-thru run of McDonald's. He ordered a Big Mac with cheese, fries, and a Coke. He chomped it down quickly to satisfy his hunger.

Griffin decided to go shopping for a badass biker's jacket and helmet. He checked for the closest store on his GPS. Siri gave him Moto Works of Chicago on South Western Avenue. He followed the familiar GPS voice, and soon he arrived at Moto Works. Griffin parked his car and ran into the store. A salesperson greeted him with a friendly smile.

"I'm looking for one bad, mother of a jacket for my new bike," Griffin said.

"What kind of bike?" the salesman asked.

"The Kawasaki KX 250F street bike," Griffin said.

"That's one bad, mother of a bike," the man said.

"You're telling me," Griffin replied.

"I've got just the one for you," the salesman said.

As soon as he pulled the jacket off the rack and showed it to Griffin, he knew it was the one.

"That's it, I'll take it," Griffin said.

Griffin's eyes were drawn to the black leather Kawasaki racing jacket the salesman held in his hands. It was one bad mother with bright green on the sleeves and top of the jacket, mixed with solid black and racing tags. It had a sturdy zipper in the front.

"That's $249," he said.

"No problem," Griffin said.

"What size?" the salesman asked.

"I need a medium," Griffin replied.

"Okay, here it is. Do you need a helmet?" the man asked.

"I would like the baddest mother of all helmets," Griffin said.

"Try this one," the man replied.

"You're not kidding; that is badass," Griffin said.

Griffin had to have that helmet. It screamed, "Take me home." Most of the helmet was covered in a bright sea-green color with black trimming. It had an anti-scratch face shield with a hard-coated 3D shield design. It was lightweight and was RST mirrored.

"How much?" Griffin asked.

"Ninety-nine dollars plus tax," the man said.

"I'll take it," Griffin said.

"You're going to fit the part," the salesman said.

"You think so?" Griffin asked.

"I know so. That'll be $382," the salesman said.

Griffin pulled four, one-hundred dollar bills out of his pocket.

The salesman gave Griffin his change with the receipt.

"Thank you," Griffin said as he hurried to his car parked outside.

The weekend was getting ready to start. Griffin was ready with his new jacket, jeans, helmet, and his kicks.

"Weekend, here I come."

***

When I looked back at this chapter, I realized how badly my heart was hurting at the time from the way I'd been bullied by Rocky and Bull Dawg at William Fentress High. I still couldn't put my father's cruel treatment behind me. I tried so hard to substitute pleasure for pain. I wanted to be accepted by this world. I was seeking acceptance, recognition, and attention from my parents through the show I was putting on, when all I really needed was love.

CHAPTER TWENTY-ONE
SHOWING OFF MY NEW BIKE

"Where are you going dressed like that?" Griffin's mom asked.

"I'm going out with my new bike. Maybe make some friends. Mom, I'm eighteen now, so you don't need to worry about me," Griffin replied.

Silence filled the room. It was an awkward moment for Griffin.

What's up with Mom? For the past eighteen years she hasn't cared or noticed what I'd wear. Now she's starting to show her concern, Griffin thought.

"Wow look at you; you're something with that jacket and helmet," she said.

"Thanks, Mom, thought you'd never notice," Griffin replied.

"Why would you say that, Sweetheart? I noticed. Your new motorcycle is awesome," his mom said.

She noticed alright. Maybe she took a two-second glance at it. But I can guarantee she didn't notice all the details, Griffin thought.

"Thanks, Mom."

Griffin walked over to her and gave her a warm hug with a kiss.

"You were smart to not get the Mustang. The bike didn't cost nearly as much, and you still have quite a bit of money left in your account," Griffin's mom said.

"You're right, Mom. The bike is a lot more fun," Griffin answered.

"Sorry your dad couldn't see this. He had to work today till five. I wish he didn't have to work on Saturdays," she said.

"I wish he were here too," Griffin said.

I wonder what Dad would have thought about it. Would he have something negative to say?

"So, you're not staying for dinner?" Griffin's mom asked.

"No, Mom, I'll be out for a while."

"Okay, have fun. See you when you get here," his mom said.

"I will, Mom, bye," Griffin said as he closed the front door.

Griffin jumped the flight of the front steps to the sidewalk and closed the gate behind him. He mounted his brand-new Kawasaki parked by the curb. He was raring to go. He put his badass helmet on, fired up the engine, and headed to the mall. He took South Oakenwald Street to the first stop sign and passed the playground till he reached the second stop sign where Griffin turned right and continued on South Oakenwald Street. He turned left onto South Lake Park Avenue and turned left into the mall. The parking lot was covered with people Griffin's age. Some were standing around their bikes and cars. Some were sitting on the hoods and bumpers. They were laughing and having a good time.

Griffin circled his bike around a group of dudes and slowed down. They were dressed in tees and cut-offs. Some were wearing baseball caps, and some were wearing shades. They stopped what they were doing and walked over to give Griffin high fives and fist bumps.

"What's up, bro?" a kid asked.

"Badass bike," another kid said.

"Bad jacket and helmet," a girl said.

Griffin didn't recognize any of the dudes there. But there was one hot-looking girl, standing alone, who strutted up to Griffin in a slow, seductive manner. He had seen her in the hallway a few times at school. Griffin thought they had Spanish class together for one semester. She had long, brown, shoulder-length hair, knock-out green eyes, and wore tight, cut-off jean shorts.

"Hey, Griffin," she said with a flirty smile.

How did she know my name? Griffin thought.

Griffin didn't know her name. He was trying hard to be cool and play hard-to-get. But inside, Griffin was nervous and shy. He was not used to hot-looking girls flirting with him.

"Are you gonna let me ride?" she asked.

"Of course," Griffin replied.

"I'm Taylor," she said.

She slightly swayed her body from side-to-side and played with her long brown hair.

"Weren't we in Spanish class together?" Griffin asked.

"Si, good memory," she replied and giggled.

Griffin's memory came back to him. He remembered Taylor, the pretty girl with long brown hair who sat at the desk beside him, smiled at him, and sent him notes during class. At the time, Griffin never thought anything more about her other than the possibility of being a friend. Griffin's shyness started to set in. He wasn't sure what to say next.

"What are you up to these days?" Taylor asked.

"I finished school," Griffin said. "How about you?"

"Yes, I graduate this year," Taylor answered.

Griffin was at a loss for words and did not know what to say next. He fumbled for the right words.

"Do I get to ride now?" she asked.

"Yes, hop on," Griffin replied.

Taylor mounted the bike and held onto Griffin's body like she'd never let go. He kept the bike idling. He felt like Taylor was putting the moves on him. He pretended to be cool. But, inside, he was trembling with nervousness. Griffin had never had a girl come onto him like that before. He wasn't sure how to act. In fact, Griffin had never had a girlfriend period. She was moving fast and coming onto him strong.

"Where did you get this badass bike?" she whispered into his ear.

"Got her at the Acme Cycle Shop."

"Dude, you must be rich," she said.

"I did come into some money recently," Griffin replied.

"Did you rob a bank?" she asked jokingly.

"No, I sold my first novel," Griffin said.

Taylor's hands were all over him as she pressed her body tightly against his backside. The soft touch of her fingers against his face made him shiver. She seemed to want Griffin's affection.

"How much did you get for your novel?" she asked.

And she was one nosy girl too.

"One hundred grand, "Griffin replied.

"Shut up. A hundred grand, for real?" Taylor asked.

"For real," Griffin replied.

"Dude, a hundred grand is a lot of money," she said.

"I've got a book tour planned for next September, too," he said.

"Look at you, a book tour. You're going to be famous," Taylor said.

"I'm planning a book launching party at the end of May. You're invited," Griffin replied.

"Wow, Dude, a book party," she said.

The more Griffin talked about his book, and his tour, the closer Taylor drew to him as if she owned him.

"I wish your party was tomorrow," she whispered.

Griffin laughed at Taylor's sense of humor.

"That would be impossible to put together by tomorrow," Griffin said.

Suddenly, Taylor and Griffin ran out of words to say. The loud noise of the bike being revved up and the chatter of the crowd grew prominent. Taylor held Griffin tighter than before. She was wearing gardenia-scented perfume. Every time Griffin took a whiff of the fragrance, it stirred his desire.

"Let's go somewhere far away from here," she whispered with a sexy, sultry voice.

Her bright, red voluptuous lips were pressed tightly against Griffin's ear and face.

Griffin revved up the engine as she held on firmly. He peeled out of the parking lot at lightning speed. Griffin felt the heat of Taylor's sizzling body seep through her shirt and shorts. It sent heatwaves through his entire body. Griffin was so ready to impress her that he did his first wheelie. She laughed and pulled herself closer into his body. Taylor and Griffin ignited a love affair.

Griffin knew the night was going to end well. They were just getting started.

CHAPTER TWENTY-TWO
BOOK LAUNCH PARTY OR NOT

Griffin and Taylor ended up taking a longer ride than expected. They drove to a secluded, wooded area on the lake in a town he was unfamiliar with.

Griffin and Taylor started kissing. They kissed until their lips were raw and made out on the sandy beach. No one was around. It was an awkward scene for Griffin, because he had never had a girlfriend before. He was still a virgin. He wasn't sure how to kiss properly or what to do when making out. He was one nervous wreck. But Taylor was confident. Somehow, she could tell it was Griffin's first time to make love. Taylor was tender and patient with Griffin. She affectionately stroked his face and neck with her fingers, whispered passionate words in his ears, and showed Griffin how to make love for the first time. They ended up sleeping naked together on the sand. She slept with her head on his bare chest with her arms around him and her bare breasts pressed closely against Griffin.

It's a wonder no one saw them. It's amazing the cops didn't stop them. Griffin woke up with the early sunlight piercing his eyes. He had a giddy smile on his face. Taylor's face lit up with a radiant glow. She moved over on top of Griffin's body and stared into his eyes with a knowing, inviting look. Taylor wrapped her naked body around Griffin's and ended up making sweet, passionate love once more before they got dressed and headed back to town on Griffin's bike. Griffin drove Taylor to her house on his bike. They traded kisses back and forth along the way. He was flying high over his newly formed relationship with Taylor. Taylor seemed to be loving every minute of his affection.

***

Griffin got back to his house around eight a.m. Sunday morning after taking Taylor to her place. He decided he would sleep in after spending the night with Taylor. It's funny how his parents didn't ask any questions or ask where he had been. They smiled at Griffin when he got up at eleven a.m. to have some late breakfast.

"Did you make any new friends yesterday?" his mom asked.

"You could say that," Griffin replied.

"What did they think of your bike?" his dad asked.

"They thought I was rich," Griffin said.

"You are rich in many ways. You're very fortunate to be able to use your gift of writing to make a living and at such a young age," his mom said.

"Your mother and I have no doubt that you will become very successful in your writing, and perhaps you'll be able to make a full-time living out of it for years to come," his dad said.

I was still confused as to why my dad was acting so nice to me. *Why is he acting this way? Why didn't he treat me this way years ago? All I remember is him beating me with his favorite choice of weapons—his belt,* Griffin thought.

"Thanks Mom and Dad. I appreciate your belief in me and your support. That means a lot to me."

Griffin grabbed a pop tart and some juice and sat down at the table with his parents.

"So, are you going to have a book launching party or not?" his mom asked.

"Yeah, I plan to," Griffin replied.

"Is it going to be at the Hard Rock Café?" his mom asked.

"Yes, if it all works out," Griffin replied.

"I'm not trying to nag you, but I'm sure you have to book those kinds of events very early," his mom said.

"Thanks, Mom. You're not nagging me. I got sidetracked with work, my bike, and stuff with life," Griffin said.

"It's easy to do. There are things I've put off for twenty years and still haven't done," his dad said.

Yeah, like loving your son, Griffin thought.

"I don't think I'll wait that long. My first book signing event is next September. If I'm going to throw this party, it's got to be sometime in May," Griffin said.

"And May is a very busy month with graduations, parties, recitals, and games. But it's the best time to have it. It will be hard to get anyone to attend during the summer with vacations and all," his mom said.

Just be a little more negative, Mom. Griffin thought.

"You've made your point. Tomorrow after work, I'll stop by the Hard Rock Café and work out the date and arrangements for my party. I'll know better then," Griffin said.

Griffin told his mom and dad goodbye as he headed to his ho-hum job at Home Depot. Time crawled slowly, but he was finally able to punch out at three p.m. Griffin was tired but there was something he had to do. If he left now, he could be downtown by three fifteen p.m. He found his car parked outside, jumped in, and started her up. He decided to get on I-90 and head to downtown. He took the West Ontario exit and found a parking garage near the Hard Rock Café.

Griffin walked two blocks to the Hard Rock and entered the building. Lucky for him, it wasn't busy. The manager, Mr. Cooper, happened to be standing near the door when Griffin walked in.

"I'm looking for the manager," Griffin said.

"I am the manager," Mr. Cooper replied.

"I want to book this place for a book launching party in May," Griffin said.

"I didn't catch your name," Mr. Cooper said.

"I'm Griffin Smith."

"Griffin, it's good to meet you. I can help you. Follow me to my office."

Griffin followed him to the back of the café and then up some stairs. Griffin stepped into a very cool looking office.

"Have a seat," Mr. Cooper said.

Griffin couldn't help but stare at all the gold records, signed guitars, and photos of famous people plastered all over his wall.

"Do you like them?" Griffin asked.

"Yes, I love them," Mr. Cooper answered.

"This is my favorite," he said and pointed to the vintage Martin guitar hanging on the wall. "It was signed by John Lennon."

"How did you get that?" Griffin asked.

"It was an inheritance from the store owner's dad who used to roadie for The Beetles," Mr. Cooper replied.

"Wow, that must be worth a whole lot," Griffin said.

"You're telling me. It's got to be worth over a hundred grand," Mr. Cooper replied.

Griffin's eyes grew wide. He couldn't believe that a hundred grand guitar was hanging on the wall inside the Hard Rock.

"So, what can I do for you?" Mr. Cooper asked.

"I'd like to reserve this place for a book launching party," Griffin answered.

"Whose party, and whose book?" Mr. Cooper asked.

"It's my party and my book," Griffin replied.

"You're an author? I mean you're so young," Mr. Cooper said.

"Yep, it's my first. It's called *A Novel Life*, and it's being published by Sheldon House Publishers."

"Wow, that's fantastic. How many people do you expect at this party of yours?" Mr. Cooper asked.

"I never really thought about it," Griffin replied.

"It would help to have an estimate. We have space available for 45 people which would be the stage area, all the way up to renting the entire café which can hold up to 700 people," Cooper said.

"I'm not sure. Let me think about it, "Griffin said.

"Then there's the issue of money—how much space can you afford?" Cooper asked.

"Money's not a problem. I got a very large advance from Sheldon House," Griffin replied.

"Oh, I see," Cooper said.

"I would invite a few friends, some neighbors and my family," Griffin said.

"So, how many would that be?" Cooper asked.

"Between twenty-five and fifty people."

"I see. It sounds like the patio area or the mezzanine level would work well for you. The patio seats forty with maximum capacity of seventy-five and the mezzanine level seats eighty with a maximum capacity of one hundred and sixty," Cooper replied.

"Let's go with the patio area," Griffin said.

"That's a good choice because we'll have some mighty fine Chicago weather in May," Cooper said.

"Good, then let's book a date," Griffin said.

"There's only one problem. May can be solidly booked for the patio area. Let's check it," Cooper said

Mr. Cooper studied the May dates and bookings on his large calendar attached to his desk.

"Looks like the only dates available for the patio are Thursday, May 25, and Sunday, May 28, in the evening," Mr. Cooper said.

"Let's do the Sunday date," Griffin said.

"Okay, you've got it. I'll need a $250 deposit," Cooper said.

"So, how much will it cost me for the patio, food, and drinks?" Griffin asked.

"Well, since you are not twenty-one years old, the cost will be lower due to no alcohol being served. The patio rental for the evening is $1,000. With rental and the cost for food and drinks for about forty people, the total cost should be around three thousand dollars," Cooper said.

"Okay, I'll book it," Griffin said,

"Excellent. Here's the paperwork for you to fill out. I will hold this date for seventy-two hours. I will need the paperwork and $250 by then," Cooper said.

"Thanks, Mr. Cooper."

Griffin stood from his chair and shook Mr. Cooper's hand. As they headed down the stairs toward the front door, Griffin couldn't believe he had booked the Hard Rock. This was going to be one amazing party.

CHAPTER TWENTY-THREE
EDIT AND PROOFING HELL

While Griffin loved all the hype about his new bestselling novel being published, he dreaded the worst part of being a published author—editing and proofing hell.

He was stoked about his upcoming book launch party at the Hard Rock Café. Griffin knew it wasn't until May, but now the date was booked. His party would be the main topic of conversations at Thanksgiving, Christmas, and the months ahead leading up to the party and the book tour. He would have to make a whole lot of friends between now and then. But these were exciting times. Griffin was living his dream and would hopefully be successful enough with his tour to make it to the *New York Times* bestsellers list.

Thanksgiving came and Griffin was the hot topic of his family ceremonial dinner. Christmas came and, again, he was the main topic of their conversations.

Then January arrived. It was cold, windy, and snowy just like most Chicago winters. January 6 was the date Griffin wanted to forget, but he would always remember it. That was the day he received a very important email from Sheldon House Publishers.

Griffin,

We are very excited about publishing your debut novel, A Novel Life. *The scheduled publishing date is September 15. Attached is the edited copy of your manuscript. The content editor has made suggested revisions for re-writes. This is the first step in getting your book to print. Please check the editing carefully and make the necessary changes. The first draft of the manuscript*

is due from you by February 1. We look forward to
reading your revised manuscript soon.

    Best, Arnold Turnbull

Griffin was so pumped about his first book being published he didn't waste any time. He reached inside the desk drawer in his room and pulled out the original manuscript first submitted to Sheldon House. Then he downloaded the Word document of the revised manuscript Mr. Turnbull sent him. Griffin was ready to go to work. He had the day off from Home Depot, so he decided to put that time to good use.

Griffin started with Chapter One: Someone's Gonna Pay for This! As he read and compared the revised manuscript with the original, he was shocked.

"Those bastards, they changed my manuscript," Griffin said.

He read further.

"They changed my words and my story," Griffin continued talking to himself.

After reading a few chapters, Griffin couldn't take it any longer. He emailed Mr. Turnbull.

    Mr. Turnbull,
    I received your revised manuscript. I have started reading it to make revisions. My words and some of my story have been changed in the first few chapters. Why did you change some of my story? I liked it the way it was. Please reply ASAP.

    Sincerely Griffin Smith

After Griffin got that off his chest, he decided to continue to read and compare both manuscripts. It was devastating how much Mr. Turnbull had changed his manuscript. But Turnbull already knew how

Griffin would react to his email to his edits and changes. Turnbull knew his client and character well.

Griffin was having trouble concentrating because he was experiencing mixed feelings. He was down and depressed about his manuscript being changed, but his mind was also on Taylor. He thought about her and the strong feelings he had for her. Griffin couldn't get Taylor off his mind. He loved the way Taylor made him feel and he thought about seeing her again.

And concerning his manuscript, Arnold Turnbull had led Griffin to believe his manuscript was perfect the way it was written. And now, Turnbull was slicing, cutting, and changing Griffin's story any way he chose.

How could he do that?

The morning passed too quickly. It was already 12:15 p.m. and Griffin decided to take a lunch break and check his email. He didn't expect to hear from Mr. Turnbull for days. But there it was—his reply.

Griffin,

Thank you for expressing your views on your revised manuscript. We at Sheldon House believe your story and book is going to be great. Your work is brilliant. Since this is your first book ever written and published, let me educate you on the editing process. You need to be flexible with the words and story you wrote. Sure, it is your baby, but we at Sheldon House have been editing for over 50 years. We know what makes a New York Times *bestseller. You are going to need to trust us with your manuscript. While you may be upset that some of your words and story have changed, we believe the revised manuscript is much stronger than it was when we first read the original. I would like to remind you, as stated in your contract, Sheldon House has the final say on the wording and the story. Thank you.*

Best, Arnold Turnbull

Griffin read his email over again. He couldn't believe this was Turnbull's reply to his last email.

Could Mr. Turnbull be right? Is the revised manuscript more of a New York Times *bestseller than my original manuscript?* Griffin thought.

Griffin kept thinking about what Mr. Turnbull said. Sometimes thoughts of Taylor overshadowed the thoughts about his manuscript.

While I may feel down and discouraged, deep in my heart I know I must at least give Mr. Turnbull a chance, Griffin thought.

Griffin thought some more.

What's the worst that can happen if Mr. Turnbull changes my story? He seems to know what he is doing. He's had a lot of New York Times *bestsellers, so I guess I'm going to have to suck it up and trust him.*

Griffin was soon over it. He couldn't let his ego get in the way.

Who do I think I am—the greatest literary writer on this Earth? I'm still a teen.

Reality hit Griffin like being hit by a dump truck. He was a novice who got lucky selling his first book. That's who he was. He needed to accept that, so Griffin decided to yield to Mr. Turnbull and his vast amount of experience.

Editing and proofing was Griffin's least favorite thing to do. He literally despised it. He could write manuscripts all day long. But when it came to edit and proofing, that was not his passion.

Griffin forced himself to continue to read the revised manuscript. He knew he had the rest of the day and was on a deadline. And although Griffin's mind wandered back to his time with Taylor, he had to focus on getting the manuscript edited and proofed. He only had twenty-five days before the deadline. Griffin had to buckle down. God, he hated deadlines. There were deadlines in school, work, family, and now deadlines with his book.

"Get your act together and accept it, Griffin," he said to himself.

Griffin kept on reading even though he would have rather been spending his time with Taylor.

"If you can't get your butt in gear now, Griffin, how are you going to make it on the tour with all those book signings?" Griffin said. So, he hunkered down, pulled himself together, and decided that it was just him and his manuscript for the rest of the day. But before he got started, he had to call Taylor.

***

Writing this chapter made me realize how green I was—how little I knew about the book publishing business. It taught me how flexible I needed to be about edits and changes if I wanted to become a successful hit author. I learned later that there were some life and death issues where I couldn't be flexible or compromise.

CHAPTER TWENTY-FOUR
THE UNEXPECTED CALL

Griffin was ready to puke. He finally managed to force himself to read the revised manuscript three times. As much as Griffin loved the story, he had to suck it up about the changes in his story from the original.

"I didn't write this," Griffin told himself.

But his inner self kept telling him, "Be patient and objective, Griffin. This could be a huge bestseller hit for you."

Without warning, Griffin's phone rang. It was Mr. Turnbull calling.

"Griffin, my lad, how are you?"

"I'm okay, Mr. Turnbull,"

"Good, glad to hear that," Turnbull said.

Silence settled in between the two of them for a moment.

"I would like for you to meet your new manager for your book tour," Turnbull said. "How is this Thursday, two p.m. for a meeting, Griffin?"

"Works for me," Griffin replied.

"I'll send you the link. Your new manager is Toby Johnson. You'll get to meet him for the first time this Thursday. He'll meet you on the site GoToMeeting.com," Turnbull said.

"Okay, Mr. Turnbull. You've got it. Don't forget, this Thursday at two p.m. CST. Write it down," Mr. Turnbull said

Before Mr. Turnbull hung up the phone, he had an unusual question.

"Griffin, did anything out of the ordinary happen to you lately?" Mr. Turnbull asked.

Griffin paused in silence for the moment.

"Why do you ask, Mr. Turnbull?"

"Last week, I got the feeling that something was wrong," Mr. Turnbull said.

"You mean like intuition or something?" Griffin asked.

"Yes, you could say that," Mr. Turnbull replied.

"Well, as a matter of fact, last week I went to the bank to deposit the check you sent me and something bad happened," Griffin said.

Mr. Turnbull became quiet, like he knew what Griffin was about to say.

"What happened?" Mr. Turnbull asked.

"After I deposited your check, I withdrew some cash to buy something," Griffin confessed.

"How much did you withdraw?" Mr. Turnbull asked.

He waited on the edge of his seat for the answer.

Mr. Turnbull is kind of nosy, Griffin thought.

"Why does it matter how much money I withdrew?" Griffin asked.

"Because I want to know, that's why," Mr. Turnbull said, raising his voice insistently

"Well, if you must know, it was $9,000," Griffin said.

"So, what happened next?" Turnbull asked.

"I got robbed," Griffin said.

"In the parking lot?" Turnbull asked.

"Yes, in the parking lot beside my car," Griffin said.

"And you couldn't see his face because he had a gun in your back," Turnbull said.

"Yes, how did you know?" Griffin asked.

"Just a wild guess," Turnbull replied as he chuckled.

Griffin paused for a moment to ponder Mr. Turnbull's accuracy on an event which had occurred almost eight hundred miles away from New York City,

"I suppose you want to know the bank, don't you?" Griffin said jokingly.

"Bender Bank," Mr. Turnbull replied.

"How in the world did you know the bank name?" Griffin asked.

Mr. Turnbull chuckled as his spoke.

"I have the cancelled check from Bender Bank with your autograph on it," Turnbull said.

"That explains it; I thought you were a prophet or something," Griffin said as he nervously laughed.

"I am sorry to hear that you got robbed, Griffin. I am glad you are safe and didn't get hurt," Mr. Turnbull said.

"Thank you, Mr. Turnbull," Griffin replied.

"Did you get my last email on my explanations of editing and changing a manuscript?" Mr. Turnbull asked.

"Yes, I did sir. I am fine with it," Griffin said.

You dumbass. You know you're not fine with it. Why did you tell him that? Griffin thought.

Turnbull paused for a second in silence and then answered.

"Have a good day, Griffin, talk to you later," Mr. Turnbull said as he hung up.

***

Everything I had described about my bank withdrawal and robbery was accurate to the penny. Still it could have been a coincidence. I had no idea that Mr. Turnbull had made two changes to my story. The other change Turnbull made in his manuscript had not yet come to pass.

After writing this chapter, I became highly suspicious of Turnbull. I was losing trust in him daily. Some things didn't add up right. Turnbull wanted to know more about me than I cared for him to know. What was he up to? What were his real motives?

CHAPTER TWENTY-FIVE
MEET YOUR NEW MANAGER

It didn't take long for Thursday to arrive. All day long up until the two o'clock hour, Griffin thought about his meeting with Toby Johnson. He thought about the crazy things Johnson might ask him to do to prepare for his book tour or what his manager might expect from him on the tour. Griffin drove himself crazy anticipating what his manager might say.

Finally, two p.m. came. Griffin logged into the link Mr. Turnbull had sent and waited to see Toby face to face for the first time. All week, he had pictured his face in his mind, trying to predict what he might look like. Now Griffin was about to find out.

Next thing Griffin knew, Toby Johnson greeted him, face to face on his iPhone screen.

"Griffin, I'm Toby Johnson, your manager," he said as he smiled at Griffin.

"So, you're Toby Johnson," Griffin said.

"I most certainly am. You're looking at him—full flesh and blood," Toby said.

Toby was somewhat of a nerd. He had brown, boyish-styled hair which he parted to the right. He still had dimples and freckles left over from his childhood. He was dressed in a dark green, plaid sports coat and a bright orange bow tie.

"Do you want to be called Toby?" Griffin asked.

"You can call me Toby or TJ, which is my nickname."

"Okay, I'll call you Toby."

"First, I want to tell you that you're a fabulous author. I've read your manuscript more than once, and I'm impressed with your abilities to write. I'm honored to be working with you," Toby said.

Griffin paused in silence to think about what he just said. He smiled.

"Well, we have a lot to talk about, I hope you're not in a rush to be somewhere," Toby said.

"No, I'm good." Griffin replied.

"I'm sure you are aware of the deadlines for everything. Let me make them clear to you. The first draft of editing and proofing is due from you on February 1. Then we will send out the second draft. That is due on March 1. The final draft is due back by May 1. Are you up for the challenge?" he asked as he looked straight into Griffin's eyes.

"Yes, of course," Griffin replied.

"I heard from Mr. Turnbull that you are planning a book launch party at the Hard Rock Café in Chicago," Toby said.

"Yes, I am," Griffin answered.

"That's great. I'll be there. Anything you can do like that to get the buzz out on your book is great," Toby said.

"No worries," Griffin replied.

"We'll be doing everything we can to promote it on our end—billboards, ads, radio and television promotion, posters, social media ads, library and bookstore promotions," he said.

"Wow, that's awesome," Griffin said.

"You're awesome. We think you're worth it," Toby replied.

"Thanks," Griffin replied."

"Be sure to keep your schedule open for the summer. We will be booking you on *Good Morning America, The Today Show, The Ellen Show, Rachel Ray, The Tonight Show with Jimmy Fallon,* and the *Stephen Colbert Show.*"

"Seriously?"

"Yes, seriously."

"Wow, that's amazing."

"I'll be emailing you the itinerary for all of the shows you'll be on. By the way, all your expenses, including travel, will be paid for. Okay, now let's talk about your upcoming tour," Toby said.

"Okay, dude," Griffin replied in awe.

"Your tour starts in Chicago on September fifteenth. You'll start at the Book Cellar signing event that day. Expect a large crowd as you begin to become a household name," Toby said.

"Wow, a household name. You mean like Taylor Swift?" Griffin asked.

"Yes, like Taylor Swift. It will be an adventure, but it will also be tiring because a lot is expected of you. At each bookstore, you are always expected to be friendly and cheerful, never rude. Remember these are your fans and customers. They must be treated with the utmost respect," Toby said.

"No worries," Griffin replied.

"You will be expected to read a chapter from your new book to your audience. Then you will answer questions from your fans. After it is over, you will sign so many books that your hand and arm will hurt with cramps," Toby said.

"No problem," Griffin said.

"You say that now, but a sixty-city book tour is grueling. It can wear you down. That's where I come in. I will be your cheer team whenever you start getting down or too tired to keep going. We will stay in close contact via Facetime, phone, text, and email. Occasionally, I will be able to make in-person appearances with you. Is that all understood?" Toby said.

"Yes, sir," Griffin answered.

"Another important matter we need to discuss is your conduct. I know you're young, and you might like to party and all, but on this tour, you must always act professional. Professionalism means not partying and staying up at all hours. You'll need the proper eight hours of sleep. Also, no drinking, no smoking, no sleeping with women, and no drugs. You'll have time for all of that when the tour is up," Toby said.

Yes, Father. Does that mean I can't take Taylor with me on tour? Griffin thought.

But instead, Griffin was more professional with his language.

"Yes, sir," he said.

Toby and Griffin went silent for a moment to catch their breaths.

"I'm stoked," Griffin said.

"Great! Let's do it. We'll sell a truckload of books," Toby replied.

"Count me in," Griffin said.

***

Mr. Turnbull closely monitored Griffin's life, including his relationship with Toby. Even though Griffin didn't like Toby, later he would learn to be appreciative of him. Toby was a big help in getting Griffin's author career off the ground.

"I don't think Griffin has a clue as to what is going on," Turnbull said to himself.

Turnbull sent Griffin a manager. But the real reason Turnbull had sent Toby Johnson was to spy on Griffin and to report back to Turnbull on Griffin's whereabouts and activities. Turnbull was dying to know how accurate the manuscript he had been writing was. Was everything Turnbull had written so far true to his story? Turnbull would receive daily updates on Griffin. Griffin didn't have a clue.

CHAPTER TWENTY-SIX
MEETING MY KNOCKOUT PUBLICIST

"What a doofus Toby Johnson was. And to think I will have to work with that dude for a whole year," Griffin said to himself.

Griffin had a week to digest everything Toby discussed with him about his book tour and all the preparation needed.

Mr. Turnbull called Griffin again to tell him he would have a meeting with his publicist on Wednesday of the following week. Turnbull emphasized that each person who was working with Griffin's tour and career was a vital part of his team. They were all equally important in making the sale of the book successful.

Mr. Turnbull set up another two p.m. meeting on Wednesday via GoToMeeting.com. This time Griffin was meeting with his publicist, Scarlett Jones.

Griffin eagerly waited for two p.m. to arrive on that Wednesday. Two p.m. came and Griffin logged into GoToMeeting.com. Her face popped up on his screen.

"You must be Griffin Smith," she said with a smile.

"I am," Griffin smiled. "Are you Scarlett Jones?"

"Yes, I'm your publicist."

Scarlett Jones was sizzling hot. She was downright gorgeous— the opposite of Griffin's manager, Toby. She had a soft curvy face with magnetic green eyes. Her shoulder-length hair was curly blonde. Her name should have been Scarlett Johansson because she had voluptuous, ruby red lips and could put anyone into a trance. Griffin was staring at a hot Hollywood film star.

"Good to meet you," Griffin said.

Griffin tried to pretend to be cool and not stare too much.

"It's a pleasure to meet you, too. I've read your soon-to-be bestselling book, and you are a very convincing author," Scarlett said.

"Thank you," Griffin replied.

"Let's talk about what my role in helping you become a bestselling author is. I am your main publicist. There are other publicists who will be working on this team with me, but I'm your go-to-person contact whenever you need me." Scarlett said.

I can go to her anytime I'd like, huh? Griffin thought.

"That's good to know," he said.

I'm trying to be cool, but I could fall all over her, Griffin thought. *What's wrong with you Griffin, you've already got a hot girlfriend, Taylor.*

"You'll need to send me information about yourself. If you write up a short bio of yourself with your age, birthdate, where you went to school, your contact information, your website, and your web address, that would be most appreciated," Scarlett said.

"I don't have a website," Griffin replied.

"Not even a social media site?" Scarlett asked.

"No, I don't," Griffin said.

"Well, then I need to take care of that. I'll arrange a photo shoot for you in town. And then I'll build you a really cool author website once you email me the short bio of yourself," Scarlett said.

"Wow, that's going to be awesome," Griffin said.

Griffin's mind ran wild with pictures of an awesome-looking website with his name, Griffin Smith, author, flashing with glitter and gold.

"Yes, it will be. The website will be where all your fans visit to follow you on your tour. I will also develop a social media presence for you on Facebook, Instagram, Snapchat, Pinterest, and Twitter. Hopefully, you will be followed by millions," Scarlett said.

"Did you say millions?" Griffin asked.

"I sure did. We have big plans for you. After we're finished with you, your name will become a household name as an author," she said.

Griffin's mind returned to a visual of what a website of a famous author would look like followed by millions of people.

"Wow, I had no idea what I was getting into," Griffin said.

"Yes, Griffin, you're a superstar author. It's time you realized that. This isn't going to be your one and only book. You'll be writing many more, I'm sure. Did I mention YouTube?" Scarlett asked.

"YouTube?" Griffin asked.

"Yes. I plan on setting up your own channel where we can make videos of you sharing your book with your fans," Scarlett said.

"That's awesome," Griffin replied.

"You'll have a chance to talk directly with your fans about whatever you want to talk about," Scarlett said.

Griffin visualized in his mind talking with his fans face to face.

"Wow, I love it," he said.

"I also need to know what days you are free for the next eight months before you start your tour," Scarlett said.

"No problem, I'll send you my schedule, Griffin replied.

"I'm currently planning a television and radio tour for you. Toby Johnson and I will set it up," Scarlett said.

"What does that involve?" Griffin asked.

"You being free for the radio and television interviews we're about to book. And, of course, you'll need plenty of sleep so you don't get sick. We'd hate to have to cancel some important show because you got sick or were too tired to be on the show. You'll need to look refreshed and energetic at all times," Scarlett said.

"*Saturday Night Live* is my favorite. Do you think I can get on that show, too?" Griffin asked.

Griffin imagined himself as the host standing in front of the live audience and cameras before millions and saying, "Live from Saturday Night." Then Griffin came back to Earth to hear Scarlett praise him.

"Of course, you can, Griffin. You can do anything you put your heart and mind to. You are a superstar; don't you ever forget that," Scarlett replied.

***

What Toby Johnson didn't learn about me, Scarlett Jones did. Mr. Turnbull had an effective spy system going. He had provided me with a manager and a publicist. Turnbull sought out every little detail of my life to compare it with the story he had written.

CHAPTER TWENTY-SEVEN
FROM PHOTO SHOOT TO CATASTROPHE

It was less than twenty-four hours before Griffin got another call from Scarlett Jones. This time she called him on his cell phone. Talk about someone who gets things done—this woman was a human work machine. She had already lined up Griffin's photo session. If this was any indication of what Scarlett was going to be like when they did the tour, Griffin was in for a serious, grueling tour schedule.

"How are you Griffin?" Scarlett asked.

"I'm alright," he replied.

"Well, I've got super news for you. I've already lined up your photographer for your photo session. Her name is Tina Tompkins. She wants to shoot you this Friday at three p.m. How is that?" Scarlett asked.

"No worries, I can be there," Griffin said.

"Fine, I will text you her studio address in downtown Chicago," Scarlett said.

"Will you be there?" Griffin asked.

"I've got a tight schedule this Friday, but I am going to try to be there for at least some of the session," Scarlett said.

Things would be so much better with you there, Griffin thought.

"I hope you'll be there," Griffin said.

"I surely hope so, too. Count on me being there, but if something comes up, I will certainly text you. Got to run," she said as she hung up.

About an hour later, Griffin got a call from his photographer.

"Is this Griffin Smith? This is Tina Tompkins. I will be shooting your photo session Friday at three p.m.," she said.

"What time will it end?" Griffin asked.

"We'll have you out in time for dinner. So, count on about six p.m. Be sure to bring several changes of clothes. Bring some solid-colored shirts like white, purple, red, or green," she said.

"No problem. I got them," Griffin said.

"Be there on time. My studio is at 862 West Buena Avenue in downtown," she said.

"Okay, thanks, I'll be there," Griffin replied.

Friday came faster than Griffin ever expected. He gathered his different colored shirts and stuffed them into a bag. He didn't want to do the photo session, but he realized how important it was for the author image.

Scarlett's going to be there, Griffin thought.

The thought of his publicist being at the session was a motivator because Griffin really liked her.

It was already two p.m., and Griffin knew it took at least forty minutes to get there with traffic. He had invited Taylor to the photo session, so he grabbed his jacket and two helmets and told his mom goodbye. Griffin fired up his Kawasaki bike and headed to Taylor's place to pick her up. Taylor was waiting for him by the curb in front of her house. When Griffin arrived, Taylor threw her arms around him and gave him a great big kiss. Taylor fastened the extra helmet over her head, hopped on the bike, and held his body tightly with both arms as Griffin sped off toward town.

Griffin made it in record time and found a parking spot on the street across from the studio on West Buena Avenue. He grabbed his bag, helped Taylor off the bike, and walked the sidewalk with Taylor to the entrance of an older, yellow-brick apartment building. Griffin opened the black, heavy metal door as he and Taylor walked the black and white octagon-shaped tile floor to where he found mailboxes for each tenant. Griffin found the name, Tina Tompkins, photographer on the mailbox which said 401 and pushed a button to ring her studio.

"This is Griffin Smith and I have my girlfriend with me, Taylor."

"Come on up, I'm ready," she replied.

129

Griffin and Taylor walked the four flights of stairs to the fourth floor and found her apartment. Griffin knocked on the door and waited.

The door opened and a tall, lanky brunette woman dressed in denim-overall, jumpsuit cut-offs, a black and white striped T-shirt, and stylish sunglasses greeted them. An aura of mystery followed her as she led Griffin and Taylor into her place.

"I'm Tina. You must be Griffin and Taylor," she spoke with a deep, breathy voice.

"Yes, I'm Griffin and this is my girlfriend, Taylor."

"Go ahead and get changed into a shirt you want to wear for the first shoot," Tina said.

Her long index finger pointed to the bathroom for Griffin to change. Tina was all businesslike and seemed to want to get the photo shoot done without chatting. Taylor helped Griffin choose the first shirt to wear from the bag he brought. Taylor leaned patiently by the bathroom door and waited for Griffin to change.

When Griffin opened the door, Tina directed him to the photo set which was set up in the far corner of her living room. Griffin sat on the stool in front of the props. Taylor helped Griffin adjust his shirt collar and fix the stray strands of his hair as Tina adjusted the lighting. Tina removed the lens cover on her camera and was ready to shoot. She removed her sunglasses and asked Taylor to stand behind her. She was unusually quiet as her eyes were concentrating on how to the make the shoot the very best.

Before Tina could start the session, her intercom buzzed.

"Tina, this is Scarlett. I'm running late."

"Okay, come on up. We're just getting started," Tina replied.

Tina opened the door to greet Scarlett.

"Hello, my darling," Tina said as she greeted Scarlett with a smile and a kiss on the cheek.

Scarlett returned the smile and kiss. Griffin walked toward the foyer to greet her.

"Griffin, so good to meet you in person. Who might this be?" Scarlett asked.

"She's my girlfriend, Taylor."

"Taylor, so glad you could come to the photo shoot," Scarlett said.

"Me too," Taylor replied.

The photo shoot went smoothly for Griffin because Tina was an experienced professional in every way. Tina made the time go by quickly, so the shoot didn't seem boring or laborious. She knew what she was doing, and she coaxed Griffin into posing in every angle with different changes of shirts. Scarlett stayed for about thirty minutes to lend her support and then had to leave due to a pressing schedule. Taylor was Griffin's biggest supporter, and Griffin was glad he had brought her to the session. Her charm and charisma brought out the best in Griffin. She made the three-hour photo shoot fun with her humor and jokes.

The clock at Tina's place said it was 5:45 p.m. They finished early. Griffin and Taylor were ready to unwind, and they were both getting tired and hungry. Griffin thanked Tina for her time and expertise and said goodbye. As they walked the apartment stairs out to the street, Griffin asked Taylor if she'd like to get something to eat with him at the Shake Shack on South Michigan Avenue. Taylor's face lit up with joy over going on a date with Griffin to Shake Shack. Taylor said she loved the food there and that she wanted to spend more time with Griffin. She told Griffin he made her feel special and needed. Griffin treated Taylor like a princess, and she told him how it made her feel all warm inside her heart and soul. They hopped on the bike, and Taylor held onto Griffin with both arms like she'd never let him go. Griffin adored her attention and affection. They pulled away from the curb and headed on South Michigan Avenue toward Shake Shack with the steady wind blowing against their faces and through their hair. For the moment, Griffin and Taylor didn't have a care in the world. They were two teens living it up, free as two birds soaring in the sky. They were laughing, touching, and kissing and so into themselves they were not paying attention to the world around them.

As Griffin passed through the intersection of South Michigan and East Jackson Boulevard, a fast-moving car suddenly ran through the red light. The driver didn't see Griffin's bright green Kawasaki and hit his bike sideways causing Griffin's body to fly up into the air some twenty feet and to land on the hood of a parked car nearby. Taylor's body flew up into the air and landed inside the flatbed of a pickup truck parked close to where Griffin's body landed. Several bystanders on the sidewalk rushed to assist Taylor and Griffin. The emergency vehicles and police sped to the scene. When the paramedics arrived, they checked Taylor and Griffin's vitals. Miraculously, they were still conscious and were alive. Paramedics carefully placed their bodies on stretchers and rushed them to ER.

***

Could this have been the work of Arnold Turnbull? Could this have been what Mr. Turnbull was referring to when he asked Griffin if anything else out of the ordinary had happened to him?

I couldn't prove it, but it was mighty suspicious.

CHAPTER TWENTY-EIGHT
DEVINE INTERVENTION?

It was a miracle, an absolute miracle that defied all reasoning. Griffin and Taylor were still alive after being hit sideways by a fast-moving vehicle at the intersection. Most victims of accidents where bodies flew into the air twenty feet and landed on parked cars do not survive. Griffin's new Kawasaki bike was totaled and twisted like a pretzel. But Griffin and Taylor were meant to live; there was no other explanation as to why they were still alive on this planet. After Griffin's parents and Taylor's mom heard the devastating, unexpected news, they rushed to the ER of Mercy Medical Center on Michigan Avenue. Griffin was in ER room six, and Taylor was in room four.

Griffin's mom threw her arms around Griffin when her eyes caught the sight of Griffin lying in the hospital bed with IVs and monitors attached to him. His dad stood in the background and observed quietly.

"Oh, Sweetheart, I am so glad you're alive," Griffin's mom said.

Griffin tried to smile but his body was in too much pain. He nodded his head to acknowledge his mom and dad's presence. She stood by Griffin's bed and held his hand anxiously waiting for a doctor or nurse to tell her about her son's condition. After about forty minutes, a tall, handsome man dressed in a white coat, wearing dark-framed glasses and carrying a tablet entered the room. He checked Griffin's vitals, and he read from his tablet.

"Are you Griffin's doctor?" his mom asked.

"Yes, I'm Doctor Farrar. You must be Griffin's mom and dad," he said.

"I'm Phyllis Smith and this is Griffin's dad, Ian." she replied. "How is my son?"

"First of all, he's going to make it. I can't explain why your son is still here other than it's a miracle he's alive after being hit by a car, falling twenty feet in the air, and landing on a car hood," Dr. Farrar said.

"Oh, dear God, it is a miracle," she replied.

"What's more amazing is your son didn't break a bone in his body and didn't suffer any internal injuries. How do you explain that? Divine intervention?" Doctor Farrar asked.

At that very moment, Phyllis Smith closed her eyes, and traced a symbol of a cross over her heart with her right hand. She spoke softly. "Thank you, Jesus," she said.

Dr. Farrar waited until she was finished with her prayer.

"He is severely bruised and will take some time to heal. But, Mr. and Mrs. Smith, your son is going to make it,"

Phyllis continued the mantra of a three-word prayer.

"Thank you, Jesus, thank you, Jesus, thank you, Jesus."

Dr. Farrar smiled at Phyllis and Ian as he closed the door behind him.

***

Two doors down from where Griffin lay in his hospital bed, Taylor was lying in bed all gauzed up, wired with IVs and monitors; and her left leg was in traction. Taylor's mom stood next to her daughter's bed and held her hand.

"Sweet Angel, I love you so much," her mom said. "You've got to pull through, Baby."

Taylor's mom tenderly rubbed her daughter's right hand. Taylor smiled but didn't answer. Her mom watched as a nurse checked Taylor's vitals. Dr. Farrar, the ER doctor on call, opened the door to Taylor's room and checked with the nurse on Taylor's condition. He wrote down some stats on his tablet.

"Are you Taylor's mom?" Dr. Farrar asked.

"Yes, I'm Ginger Barnes," she replied. "Is my baby going to make it?"

"I'm Dr. Farrar," he said. "Yes, your daughter's going to make it."

Ginger let out a joyous laughter and raised her hands toward the ceiling.

"Thank God," Ginger said.

"It's going to be a while before she is discharged. She'll need some time to heal. Your daughter has a punctured lung, three broken ribs, and a severely fractured leg and pelvis."

"But you said she would make it, didn't you?" Ginger asked.

"Yes, I stand by my prognosis. Your daughter will make it."

"Hallelujah," Ginger shouted.

Again, Ginger raised her hands and arms dramatically toward the ceiling.

"Your daughter is one lucky girl. I can't think of anyone who has survived an accident like hers. She fell at least twenty feet after being hit by a car to land inside the flatbed of a truck," Dr. Farrar said.

"Unbelievable. Thank God she is alive," Ginger said.

"Yes, she is alive. But she will need several surgeries and could be in the hospital for four to six weeks. But with the proper treatment, she will return to her everyday activities," Dr. Farrar said.

"Thank you, Doctor," Ginger said.

She hugged Dr. Farrar with both arms as tears rolled down her face.

Griffin was discharged from Mercy Medical Center first as he only had to spend three days in the hospital. He was still sore but was able to move around and even drive his old Breeze after a week of recovery. But for the next five weeks, Griffin visited Taylor in her room at Mercy Hospital every day. He brought her balloons, cards, flowers, and books to read while she was recuperating. Part of Griffin felt guilty for Taylor ending up in the hospital with severe injuries. Another part of Griffin suspected Mr. Arnold Turnbull had something to do with the tragic accident. It would be difficult to prove, but Griffin had to find out by asking Turnbull some tough questions.

***

This was a tough chapter to write especially about the accident and Taylor's terrible injuries. My emotions were running high. I was angry at whoever or whatever caused the accident to happen. My mind kept going back to Turnbull. What did he mean when he said he controlled my destiny?

CHAPTER TWENTY-NINE
I NEED AN ANSWER

Griffin was about to call Mr. Turnbull when Turnbull beat him to it.

"Griffin, this is Mr. Turnbull," the voice said on the other end of the line.

"Mr. Turnbull, I haven't talked to you in a while," Griffin replied.

"I'm calling to remind you that your first edited draft is due in a few days. I haven't received it yet."

"Oh, that's because I've been busy," Griffin said.

Griffin tugged at his hair in frustration and gritted his teeth. He felt stressed.

"How have you been, young lad?" Turnbull asked.

"Not so good; I've had a turn of bad luck," Griffin said.

"What's wrong, Griffin?" Turnbull asked.

"I had a bad motorcycle accident," Griffin said.

Turnbull stopped talking for a moment in silence. Then he replied.

"I'm so sorry," Mr. Turnbull said. "What happened?"

"My girlfriend, Taylor, and I were on my Kawasaki headed to get something to eat when a car ran the light and hit us in the side"

"Seriously, unbelievable. What happened next?" Turnbull asked.

"The force of the car slammed Taylor and me up nearly twenty feet into the air. We both landed on vehicles parked nearby. EMTs rushed us to the ER," Griffin said.

"And you lived to tell about it. How is your girlfriend?" Turnbull asked.

"Taylor has three broken ribs, a punctured lung, a severely fractured leg, and a broken pelvis," Griffin said.

"How long will Taylor have to spend in Mercy Medical Center?" Turnbull asked.

Griffin paused in silence to think about what Turnbull had just said. He felt sick to the pit of his stomach.

"How did you know Taylor was in Mercy Medical Center? I never told you," Griffin said.

"Uh, uh, uh, I just know it's the best hospital in Chicago," Turnbull said as he stuttered to get the words out of his mouth.

Griffin paused again in silence.

"Mr. Turnbull, is there something you're not telling me?" Griffin asked.

Turnbull didn't answer Griffin's question. Silence stood in the way of their conversation for a few seconds.

"Mr. Turnbull, do you remember asking me a few weeks ago if anything out of the ordinary happened to me?" Griffin asked.

Turnbull remained silent.

"Then you asked me if anything else happened. At the time, the only thing that happened was the robbery. Nothing else happened to me until Taylor and I got hit by a car," Griffin said.

Turnbull ignored Griffin's questions and changed the subject.

"I am sorry to hear about you and Taylor having that accident. I hope you will be feeling better. Look forward to receiving your first draft edits," Mr. Turnbull said as he hung up the phone.

A nagging intuitive feeling from the pit of Griffin's stomach wouldn't leave Griffin alone. That strange feeling told Griffin something wasn't right about the whole situation with Turnbull and the terrible events which recently occurred in his life.

***

Eight hundred miles away in the offices of Sheldon House Publishers, Arnold Turnbull was laughing and all smiles. He had finally received his answer and affirmation about the chapters he had recently changed in *A Novel Life*. Every detail, word and action were exactly how he had written it. Turnbull could confidently say, without a doubt, he could control every word and action of Griffin and the other characters in his manuscript. Turnbull could even re-write Griffin's fate. Mr. Turnbull marveled at the power he held in his hands and fingers. With just the touch of some keystrokes he could make or break Griffin. Turnbull could change anything he damn well liked to. He was the master of Griffin. Knowing what Turnbull knew now gave him a license to plot and scheme about different angles his book could take. Griffin's life would be full of surprise. Griffin just didn't know it yet.

***

I began to learn how evil and manipulative Turnbull was. What kind of person would want to change someone's story into tragedy? What would be their motive?

CHAPTER THIRTY
MY BOOK LAUNCHING PARTY

It was finally over. Griffin could now sleep and breathe again.

The months leading up to his long-anticipated book launch party were spent editing and proofing his new novel. It was unbelievable the long hours spent and the few hours of sleep he got. Griffin absolutely loved the creative process of writing every word of his book, but when it came time to editing and proofing, he would have rather had a root canal than to face the torture of editing and proofing.

The winter and spring months were rough after being robbed and then almost losing his girlfriend and his life in a horrible motorcycle accident. Griffin spent time recuperating as well as spending every waking day visiting Taylor until she was discharged from the hospital.

But finally, all the editing and proofing was done. Griffin made all his deadlines. The galley of his book was about to be released just in time for his book launch party. His publisher explained to him that a galley was an advanced copy of the book meant for reviews by other authors or editors. Sheldon House Publishers would collect reviews so they could place quotes or blurbs on the front, back, or inside of the book.

It was getting close to Griffin's party date of May twenty-eighth. It would be here in just a few weeks. Griffin sent all his invites on social media to business acquaintances and the few acquaintances he had made in high school and some of Taylor's friends that he had met. Griffin's mother insisted he mail out card invitations by U.S. mail, but Griffin told her no one did that anymore. He explained to her the way to get people to his party would be set up a book event on Facebook and to send out invitations on other social media along with emails. Griffin also planned on sending text reminders a day before the party.

Griffin's mom helped him choose the food items the Hard Rock Café would serve during his party. They decided on pizza, miniature burgers, soda, and bottled water since Hard Rock Café was not allowed to serve alcohol to minors. The adults attending would have to suck it up. Some musicians Griffin met a few months ago had an Indie rock band, so he contacted them to see if they were available to play. Griffin was pumped to learn they would be playing for his party. They were doing him a favor and decided to only charge him one grand to play that evening for two hours. Griffin had the money and was glad to help them. Besides, the band was good and would make an impression on his guests.

Griffin's parents and Griffin weren't exactly sure how many people they would be expecting. The Hard Rock Cafe told them the patio area could accommodate up to sixty people. They sent over eighty invitations but figured they'd be lucky if they got even half of those invited to attend, particularly in May as there were so many events they were competing with. Griffin took his mom's advice and tried to make some friends along the way. If anything, they were more like acquaintances or business associates than friends. A few of those might show, but most guests would be neighbors, and family. Griffin had a large family of cousins, nephews, aunts and uncles, and grandparents.

The weeks passed. Now it was only one week before the party. Griffin's parents were concerned because they had only heard from a few people who had RSVP'd. Perhaps not as many people would show.

Were they not excited about their homeboy signing a major book deal?

The day before Griffin's party, his parents received more RSVPs, but still not enough. Griffin and his mom figured they'd have fifteen or twenty guests if they were lucky. They were stumped on what to tell Hard Rock Café about how much food they would need. It was far better to have more food available than to run short should they have a larger crowd. They decided to tell the Hard Rock Café to prepare to serve at least forty people. It turned out their optimism was correct.

***

Sunday, May twenty-eighth had finally arrived. It was the day Griffin had anxiously waited for all these months. His dad and mom dressed like Griffin hadn't seen them dress since his baptism. Ian wore a navy-blue suit, blue oxford dress shirt, and a red necktie. Phyllis wore a new, long yellow-floral-print dress. Her hair was styled with curls especially for Griffin's event. His parents were extremely proud of Griffin and showed it too. But even two years ago, they wouldn't have given him the time of day. As for Griffin, he wanted to look cool and dress like a young cool author. He decided to wear his leather biker's jacket, jeans, shades, and boots. No one would be able to accuse Griffin of being a nerd—never. And though from time-to-time, flashbacks of the horrific bullying at William Fentress High still haunted Griffin's memory, the process of writing his book and the journey to become an author became therapeutic. Griffin's writing brought him closer to his dad and mom. His painful memories of being beaten by his dad and ignored by his mom still lingered in his mind but were gradually being replaced with more positive feelings toward his parents.

Griffin's party wasn't supposed to start until seven p.m. but he arrived early at six p.m. with Taylor holding onto his arm. It was truly a miracle Taylor was alive after she had fully recovered from three broken ribs, a punctured lung, three surgeries, and a severely fractured leg and pelvis. Taylor was a sight to see in her fashionable red miniskirt and red silk, sequined top. She wore her hair curled, pearl bracelets, a necklace, and black high heels. She even wore Griffin's favorite gardenia-scented perfume. Griffin's nose recognized that familiar scent. Taylor held onto Griffin proudly as if she owned him. And to Griffin's surprise, his publisher had been working overtime. A giant color banner stretched between the building and the balcony railing posts: CONGRATULATIONS AUTHOR, GRIFFIN SMITH! The banner had a large photo of Griffin beside the words. Griffin's eyes couldn't believe what he was seeing. A colorful, decorated table stood under the large banner displaying sample copies of Griffin's new book along with attractively designed color flyers and bookmarks advertising his signing and tour dates. Griffin's very first book signing would be held at the downtown Book Cellar store on September fifteenth.

A giant A-frame stand, which must have been at least six feet tall and four feet wide, stood to the right of the display table. Attached to it was an oversized color billboard of the front cover of *A Novel Life*. On the opposite side of the A-frame was an oversized color headshot of Griffin.

Unbelievable, Griffin thought.

The patio was decorated with streamers and balloons. A large, rectangular cake about three feet long by two feet wide which read: CONGRATULATIONS GRIFFIN ON A NOVEL LIFE was decked out on another table.

"Boy, when Sheldon House promotes, they promote," Griffin said to himself.

The band had arrived and was warming up. Then at about 6:30 p.m. guests started to arrive. And a steady crowd continued to pour in. It was overwhelming.

"This is a good sign," Griffin said to Taylor.

As the clock struck seven p.m., the band started playing and were in full party mode. Suddenly, the patio had a shoulder-to-shoulder crowd, and people were still pouring into the balcony area.

"What are we going to do about having enough food?" Griffin asked his mom.

"Don't worry, Son. I'll speak to the management about getting more food," his mom replied.

"There must be over eighty people here, and there are more trying to get inside," his dad said.

"Yep, and I hardly know anyone," Griffin replied.

It was unbelievable. The crowd was overflowing. There were a few acquaintances Griffin had met recently. Some of Taylor's friends had come. There were some family members and neighbors. But most of the crowd congratulating Griffin were strangers. He had no clue who they were. It didn't matter to Griffin. He was with his girlfriend; this was his moment, and he was having the time of his life.

With Taylor by his side, Griffin worked his way through the crowd. As he turned to the right, he caught a glimpse out of the corner of his eye of Mr. Turnbull and what looked like the entire staff at Sheldon House. Mr. Turnbull reached out to shake Griffin's hand.

"Griffin, you are the man. You are a superstar," Turnbull said.

"Thank you. I am humbled to be honored here tonight," Griffin replied.

"Who's this beautiful young lady?" Turnbull asked.

"I'm Taylor, Griffin's girlfriend," she replied.

Mr. Turnbull shook her hand. The look on his face was the look of someone who had just seen a ghost. Turnbull tried to change the subject.

He never asked how Taylor was doing. He never even mentioned the accident. He pretended to not know who she was. Something's fishy, Griffin thought.

"Can you believe all these people are here just for you?" Mr. Turnbull said.

"It's overwhelming. I just want to share the joy of having my first book published with everyone who came here tonight," Griffin replied.

"This is a very good start. Imagine the crowd you'll have at your very first book signing on September fifteenth in your hometown," Mr. Turnbull said.

"I can only imagine." Griffin replied

"Griffin, I brought your manager and publicist along. You've already met online, but they are here in person. Griffin, meet Toby Johnson and Scarlett Jones."

No, not Toby. I can't stand him.

144

"Great to meet you in person. Scarlett and I have already met," Griffin said.

Scarlett can stay. She's a keeper, Griffin thought.

Turnbull didn't introduce Taylor to them. Griffin decided to introduce her.

"This is one rocking party. We were only expecting maybe fifteen or twenty people. But it looks like way more than that," Griffin said.

"I'd say you've got an overflow crowd," Mr. Turnbull said.

"How is that possible? I don't know most of them," Griffin said.

Mr. Turnbull leaned over toward Griffin and whispered in his ear.

"I'll let you in on a little secret. Sheldon House took out full-page ads in the *Chicago Tribune* and other Chicago papers with your photo and a photo of the book cover inviting them to your party. We covered social media too. That's how we did it," Turnbull confessed.

So, Turnbull paid all these people to come to my party. Fake friends, fake fans, fake party. Griffin thought.

***

I wondered what else Turnbull was responsible for and what he could do in the future. He was bound and determined to make my party a success because he spent lavish amounts of money to make it a hit.

CHAPTER THIRTY-ONE
NO FREE SUMMER FOR ME

Finally, the summer arrived. Griffin thought he could chill with Taylor somewhere on the beach without a care in the world.

Wrong.

Griffin put his book launch party behind him. He had finished the grueling job of editing and proofing. The galleys of his book were out, and reviewers were providing glowing blurbs and quotes to decorate the front and back covers.

Summer was quickly passing him by. Griffin was about to face an exciting but tiring chapter in his life as an author on tour. Sure, he was young and up for the sixty-city tour he was about to start on September fifteenth. But he could never experience his summer freedom and time spent with Taylor once the tour started. It was already June and Griffin was counting down the days until the tour. But he had forgotten his publicist, Scarlett Jones, had scheduled a full summer of guest television and radio appearances. So much for escaping to the beach and chilling all summer with Taylor. It would be a summer of non-stop work if Scarlett had a say in it.

Griffin wasn't far off from his assessment of her. The first full week of June started with his guest appearance on the *Ellen Show*. Ellen was a riot. She had Griffin laughing in stitches. She gave away signed copies of his book and promoted Griffin to perfection. Ellen asked some difficult questions that stumped him. But, fortunately, Griffin answered them and didn't make a fool of himself. Scarlett was pleased with his appearance and told him that after the show aired, they sold a ton of pre-orders on Amazon.

The next week Griffin made his debut on the *Tonight Show* with Jimmy Fallon. Fallon was amazed that a nineteen-year-old person could write such a "masterpiece." He had a few questions that Griffin almost couldn't answer, but thanks to Scarlett's preparation, Griffin got through it.

He's got to be the funniest man alive, Griffin thought.

Griffin laughed so hard that he thought his eyeballs would explode. He laughed after he left the show and throughout the week. Jimmy Fallon was the best.

In between the television shows, Scarlett had booked a lot of radio shows. They were fun but not nearly as much fun as live television.

Before July first, Griffin was a guest on the following shows: *Late Night Show* with Stephen Colbert, *The Rachel Ray Show*, the *Today Show*, *Good Morning America*, *CBS Morning Show*, and *Fox and Friends*. There was much flying back and forth from airport to airport and hotel to hotel.

"You better get used to this," Griffin's publicist advised.

Scarlett was right, they were only getting started with the media tour. They were only one-third through all the radio and television shows Griffin was to appear on as a guest. It was an exhausting whirlwind media tour. Griffin felt like he was campaigning for president.

But all the hard work was paying off in a big way. Griffin's book wasn't due to be published until September fifteenth, but the pre-sale orders on Amazon had already passed one million. That was incredible. He'd already made over two million dollars minus his advance, and he hadn't even started touring.

Griffin became an instant millionaire at age nineteen. He was becoming a huge success. But there was one major problem. Griffin's relationship with Taylor fell by the wayside. Their relationship showed much wear and tear. Taylor had become resentful of the fact that Griffin was spending most of his time promoting his book and wasn't spending any time with her. And during the little time Griffin spent with her, Taylor became more possessive of him and very clingy. She was threatened by Griffin's obsessive need to promote the new book. Griffin missed spending time with Taylor and felt guilty for leaving her behind. Something had to give. Griffin feared he would lose Taylor.

CHAPTER THIRTY-TWO
FIRST BOOK SIGNING

Griffin was sweating tennis balls. He feared the worse. He must have paced the floor of his room hundreds of times.

"What if no one shows for my hometown book signing? "Griffin he said to himself.

Saturday, September fifteenth had arrived quickly. It was the start of Griffin's sixty-city tour. In a few hours, he would be greeting fans at the famous Book Cellar on Lincoln Avenue. Hopefully, he would have a large crowd and sell a ton of books.

Toby Johnson and Griffin had created an event on Facebook. They had forty-six people who said they were going, one-hundred-and-forty-two maybes, and fifty-five nos. If Griffin was to believe the forty-six people who claimed they were attending, he would have a pretty good crowd. But pretty good wasn't good enough. Griffin needed an enormous crowd—a standing room only with people lined out the door and into the street. Chicago was his hometown, and that should count for something.

This past year, the Book Cellar had hosted such famed authors as Judy Blume, James Patterson, David Baldacci, John Grisham, Suzanne Collins, Nicholas Sparks, and Stephen King. And now they were going to host Griffin Smith—an unknown, barely nineteen-year-old kid who'd had his first book published. It was quite intimidating having to follow those famous authors. But it was going to happen today—crowd or not.

"Let's do it," Griffin said to himself.

Griffin put on his dark blue, silk, long-sleeved dress shirt with pearl buttons and left the tails hanging out. He got into a pair of faded, light-colored ripped jeans and wore his leather biker's jacket. Griffin put on his favorite pair of Converses. He was ready.

His mom and dad had already arrived to the signing early and were waiting for him at the Book Cellar.

Griffin felt bad he hadn't spent much time with Taylor during the summer. He'd decided to ask Taylor to go with him to his first book signing. He wasn't sure how it would work out with Taylor feeling insecure and threatened by so much attention being focused on him. Still he wanted to include his girlfriend, and he appreciated her support of him. It was only an hour before the signing, but it took twenty minutes on a Saturday to get to downtown Chicago. Griffin had to stop at Taylor's place to pick her up, so he decided to leave early enough to make sure there was no chance of being late.

Griffin closed the front door and walked the sidewalk through the black iron gate to his newest green Kawasaki parked on the street. Griffin's insurance company bought him a brand-new Kawasaki as his other bike had been totaled in the accident. He took a long, deep breath.

Let's get this over with, Griffin thought.

Griffin mounted the bike, put his helmet on, and fired her up. He kicked back the kickstand and revved up the engine with the throttle. He took another long, deep breath.

"Ready or not, here I come," Griffin said to himself.

Griffin stopped at Taylor's place. Taylor looked stunning, standing on the curb waiting for him. She wore a denim miniskirt with a matching denim jacket. Her haired was curled, and she wore some large turquoise, Southwestern style earrings. Taylor hopped on Griffin's bike, fastened her helmet around her head, and held onto Griffin tightly with both hands. Griffin sped off and headed toward the I-94 entrance toward downtown. They would arrive shortly.

They reached Lincoln Ave at 1:20 p.m. Griffin hadn't anticipated a problem of having to find parking on a Saturday afternoon, yet he kept driving around the block where the Book Cellar was, searching for a free parking space. He cut down a side street and took a short cut through an alley behind some stores and came out on a street he wasn't familiar with. But Griffin found a free parking zone—and it wasn't in an illegal spot or in a towing zone. He parked right next to the free two-hour parking zone sign. Griffin hopped off his bike and helped Taylor. He put the kickstand down, grabbed Taylor's hand, and they sprinted to the Book Cellar as he had less than thirty minutes before his signing event would start. He was the one who was supposed to be on time.

Griffin and Taylor ran past the Chicago Bauhaus Restaurant, and as they turned the corner, they saw a crowd of people standing in line waiting to enter the Book Cellar.

"Oh my God, what am I going to do? Are all those people coming to see me?" Griffin asked Taylor.

Griffin and Taylor slowed down and stared, confused. They took some long, deep breaths.

"This is embarrassing. I'm supposed to be inside the Book Cellar. Not outside, fighting my way, trying to get in," Griffin said.

"Don't worry, Griffs, it'll be okay," Taylor replied.

Taylor rubbed her hand on his shoulder to reassure him and show her support.

Griffin took a few steps toward the crowd, holding Taylor's hand. They recognized him. The crowd applauded and cheered him. The people in line rushed toward Griffin as if he was a rock star.

"It's Griffin," they shouted.

Taylor appeared nervous and stopped in her tracks.

"It's okay, Taylor. Hold my hand; it will be okay," Griffin said.

The crowd started chanting.

"Griffin, Griffin, Griffin."

Griffin smiled nervously and shyly waved to them as he moved through the crowd and toward the front door, holding Taylor's hand. Griffin's hands and feet were shaking. His stomach felt uneasy.

Griffin and Taylor reached the front glass door. As they opened the door, their eyes caught a room filled with people. Griffin had never seen so many faces. It warmed his heart to feel so much love. The room was noisy with people waiting to be seated. There were not enough seats. Griffin always thought the Book Cellar was a bigger bookstore than this. Either the bookstore was small, or the crowd was gigantic.

The crowd cheered and applauded as they recognized him.

"Griffin, Griffin, Griffin," they shouted again.

It was overwhelming. Griffin was dazed and confused. He knew Taylor was feeling overwhelmed. He felt a touch on his shoulder. Scarlett Jones, his publicist had come to the rescue.

"Let's get you ready," she said with her voice raised above the noise of the crowd.

Scarlett escorted him through the chairs of people and toward the podium where he would speak. Griffin tried his best to keep Taylor by his side, but somehow, she got separated in the crowd.

Griffin's manager, Toby Johnson, rushed up to him and assisted Griffin to the podium. Griffin tried to force a smile through all the chaos.

"You will be speaking at this podium. Tell them about yourself, perhaps an interesting story on how you wrote the book, and then take questions. Be yourself, Griffin, they love you," Toby said.

Griffin stood in silence, staring out at the sea of people in the room. Every chair had been taken, and people stood in front of him, behind him, and outside on the sidewalk.

Griffin's face was dripping with sweat. He tried to wipe it. His eyes scanned the room for Taylor but he didn't see her.

"Here's a hanky," Scarlett said.

Griffin took the handkerchief from her soft delicate hands and wiped the sweat from his brow. He tried to stay calm.

"Stay calm; relax, Griffin. You can do this," Griffin told himself.

Griffin stood there frozen, staring at all the people. The noise in the room turned to silence as Mr. Turnbull rose to the podium to introduce him.

"I'm Arnold Turnbull, President and CEO of Sheldon House Publishers. I am pleased to introduce to you a very gifted, brilliant author—our youngest author yet. Remember the name, Griffin Smith. It will soon be a household word. His book has already sold over one million copies in pre-orders. Today, *A Novel Life* is now officially released. You are here to witness the official release. I proudly introduce to you, Griffin Smith."

The crowd suddenly broke into thunderous applause with cheering, which could probably be heard for blocks. Griffin was overwhelmed with the love his fans showed him. His knees shook violently. His stomach felt like it was doing Olympic-style summersaults. Griffin took a few steps to the podium and pulled the microphone toward his mouth.

The crowd's thunderous applause suddenly grew to a deafening silence.

"Hi, I'm Griffin Smith."

The crowd started up again.

"Griffin, Griffin, Griffin," they shouted.

Griffin smiled and waited for the crowd to calm down.

"I am humbled by this large crowd. Wow, I didn't know I had so many friends," Griffin said as he tried to laugh.

"We love you Griffin," a man shouted.

"Since I was five years old, I have wanted to be an author. My mom and dad say I wrote words on everything in the house—paper, my hands, toilet paper, checks, and the walls," Griffin said.

The crowd roared with laughter. They put Griffin at ease. His legs stopped shaking, and his stomach felt at peace.

"Hope you enjoy my debut book as much as I enjoyed writing it. I feel like I've lived every page. I can identify with every character in it. This is the start of my sixty-city book tour. You have made me feel welcomed and loved. I couldn't think of any finer way to kick off my tour than to spend it with you," Griffin said.

The crowd wildly applauded and cheered loudly.

"Thank you, thank you. There is someone I would like to introduce to you. She's my biggest supporter and I wouldn't be here without her. Please give it up for Taylor Barnes, my girlfriend," Griffin said.

The crowd continued to applaud wildly. Griffin scanned his eyes around the crowd to find Taylor's face.

"Taylor, wherever you are, come on up," Griffin said.

Taylor was hesitant to walk up to the podium. Her face looked flushed and she was nervous. But the crowd gently nudged her and cheered her to step forward. When Taylor reached Griffin's side, the crowd cheered and applauded hysterically. Griffin gave her a big hug to show everyone Taylor truly was his girl. Griffin flashed a wide, genuine smile as he held Taylor. He continued by thanking the Book Cellar, Arnold Turnbull, Sheldon House, his publicist, his manager, and his mom and dad.

"Thank you. Now if you have any questions, I would be glad to answer them. Afterwards, I would be glad to personally sign a book for you," Griffin said.

The crowd became silent again.

Many in the crowd raised their hands to ask questions.

"Yes, the woman in the red sweater," Griffin said as he pointed to a seat in the back.

"How did you come up with the idea for your first book?"

"Good question. I felt like I had been living a curious life all this time. I thought my life might be interesting enough to write about," Griffin answered.

"So, is *A Novel Life* about you and your life even though it's fiction?" she asked.

"You could say that. It's fiction but the idea came from a true story—my life," Griffin answered. "Another question? Yes, the man wearing the black hat," Griffin said as he pointed to the back.

"Hi, I'm Rupert Smith with the *Chicago Tribune*. Is it true your parents pulled you out of William Fentress High last year and you never returned?"

The crowd reacted negatively by booing. Griffin stood behind the podium in silence, trying to find an answer. He ignored the reporter because Griffin thought his question was too personal to answer. So, Griffin moved on.

"Next question," Griffin said as he pointed to the young woman wearing a bright yellow dress, standing in the back.

"What did you learn from writing this novel?" she asked.

154

"Good question. I learned a lot about myself—that I've been given a gift of writing and that I need to use it. I learned that writing a book is hard work. And I found out what I love the best and what I love the least. I love to create, but I despise the editing and proofing," Griffin said.

Griffin remained at the podium and answered almost every question. Taylor stood faithfully and patiently by Griffin's side. Even though Taylor felt uncomfortable standing in front of crowds, she was proud of Griffin and showed her support for him no matter how she felt.

Griffin had never seen so much interest in a book. He had never seen so many questions.

"Thank you, my friends, for coming out to support me. Thank you for showing so much love. I love you," Griffin said as he raised his voice to end his speech.

Griffin's speech ended with thunderous applause and cheers.

Scarlett Jones, Toby Johnson, and Mr. Turnbull surrounded him like the Secret Service would surround the President as the crowd rushed to shake his hand, to touch his arms and shoulders, and to speak with Griffin. Griffin's team escorted him to the front of the store where he would meet the crowd and sign his books. Griffin made sure Taylor was by his side. The crowd enthusiastically followed Griffin.

Toby Johnson announced to the crowd that if they wished to get a signed copy, they would first need to take the book to the register and pay for it. Afterwards, Griffin would sign it. The book signing part was so organized that a roped line of people stretched all around the store and out the front door onto the sidewalk. It reminded Griffin of the way they roped off lines for rides at Disney World. After Toby spoke, the Book Cellar management announced on the store intercom their policy of buying the book first and then showing the receipt for the book to be signed.

Griffin's first customer was a tall, attractive young woman who attempted to flirt with Griffin. She had a serious crush. Her eyes were dreamy looking, filled with a million stars.

"Would you sign my book, Griffin?" she asked.

"Sure, who do I sign it to?" Griffin asked.

"Me," she said.

She swayed her body from side to side with her hands nervously tucked behind her back. It appeared her face was fully flushed with a glazed, dazzled look in her eyes. Griffin felt uncomfortable with receiving flirtatious behavior from his fans. Taylor stood next to Griffin as he signed books. Griffin went out of his way to let it be known he loved his girlfriend.

"What's your name?" Griffin asked.

"Anabel."

"Spell it," Griffin said.

"A-N-A-B-E-L," she said.

"Okay, thanks."

Griffin signed her book with the message, "To Anabel, with love, Griffin Smith."

When she read his message, she fell apart. She blushed and continually laughed with a high-pitched silly laugh.

"Could I have a picture with you?" she asked.

"Sure," Griffin replied.

Griffin stood as she ran around to the back of the table and threw her arms around him as if he was a rock star or her prized boyfriend. Her girlfriend took the photo.

She kept hanging around Griffin as if she wanted more. She held up the line and kept the anxious fans waiting. Griffin paid attention to Taylor and ignored Anabel. At that moment, Toby Johnson walked around the table and whispered in Griffin's ear. He could tell Toby wasn't happy.

"You've got to keep the line moving or you're going to lose your fans and customers," he said.

What a turkey. I'm not going to hit on that woman. I've got a girlfriend, Griffin thought.

Griffin nodded his head as if he was agreeing with Toby. He wanted Griffin to spend just the right amount of time with each fan as to make them happy, but not to spend too much time on one person.

Griffin understood what he was saying even though he didn't agree with him. From then on, Griffin smiled at each fan, thanked each one for attending his book event, and then signed their book. After about eight or nine fans, he had it down pat.

It was amazing how each fan waited patiently in line to meet Griffin and get their book signed. Griffin must have signed over four hundred copies of his book. The fans kept coming and the line seemed to never stop. His hand and wrist were sore from signing so many books. Still, Griffin was having a blast. He was grateful to Taylor for being by his side for support. Griffin greeted each fan as if they were the first, down to the very last one in line.

After every fan's book had been signed, Mr. Turnbull shook their hand.

"Congratulations, Griffin, you are a hit with your fans," Turnbull said.

"Thanks, "Griffin said.

Griffin felt numb from signing so many books.

"You're going to do just fine on your tour," Turnbull said

"Thanks," Griffin replied.

"You seem a little tired," Turnbull said.

"Overwhelmed," Griffin said.

"You'll get over that," Turnbull replied.

"Thanks for the vote of confidence," Griffin said.

"I am proud of you, Griffin, and look forward to many more of these. I've got to catch a plane in less than an hour, so I'll talk to you later," Turnbull said.

"Thank you for coming out today. It means a lot to me," Griffin replied.

"I wouldn't have missed it for anything," he replied as he waved goodbye and closed the front door behind him.

At that moment, Toby Johnson and Scarlett Jones walked up to Griffin.

"Great job today, Griffin," Toby said.

"You really rocked this place," Scarlett said.

"Thanks, you guys, for coming out to my book event," Griffin said.

"I'm going to have to run," Toby said.

"Yep, we've got more to do today," Scarlett said.

"Thanks, I understand. Talk to you later," Griffin said.

Toby, you can get the crap out of here. I don't care if I ever see you, Griffin thought.

Griffin forced a fake smile at him.

Everyone else had gone. The bookstore finally cleared out except for three important people in Griffin's life—his mom, dad, and Taylor. They ran up to Griffin and gave him enthusiastic hugs and kisses.

"We're so proud of you, Son," Griffin's dad said.

"My dear baby boy, you are the love of my life. I can't say enough about how proud I am of you," his mom said.

"Thanks." Griffin blushed and looked around to see if anyone was looking.

"We'll see you later tonight, Griffin. We are headed home to get some dinner," his mom said.

Taylor waited patiently until everyone left the bookstore before she spoke a word.

Griffin and Taylor walked slowly together, hand-in-hand out of the front door of the Book Cellar. It was a nice, pleasant afternoon with a cool breeze. Then Taylor stopped in front of the restaurant next to the bookstore. She leaned her body forward against Griffin's body and looked him straight in the eyes. Tears of joy clouded her eyes. Her voice choked as she spoke her heart and mind.

"Griffin, you made me proud today. You are awesome, brilliant, and amazingly talented; I am grateful to be your girlfriend," Taylor said.

"Thank you, Taylor. That means the world to me," Griffin replied.

Taylor reached her hands and arms around Griffin and kissed him passionately.

"You being here today to support me means everything to me," Griffin said.

Taylor leaned forward and kissed Griffin again.

Griffin looked Taylor in the eyes and spoke from the heart.

"I am sorry we haven't spent much time together this summer. I'm going to make it up to you tonight by taking you to the Celeste Restaurant at Lincoln Park," Griffin said.

"Really? I heard that's an awesome restaurant," Taylor replied.

Her face lit up with excitement as her body danced with joy.

"Not only does it have amazing food, but the band Peerless is playing tonight,"

"Awesome," Taylor said.

"Tonight, we're going to celebrate and have the time of our lives. We are going to live it up," Griffin said.

***

I felt thankful for the loving and supportive girlfriend Taylor had been. It made me sad to think Taylor and I would have to put our relationship on hold because of my sixty-city book tour. My tour would be grueling and time consuming, and it would leave little time to include Taylor.

CHAPTER THIRTY-THREE
THE TOUR BEGINS

Taylor didn't waste any time letting Griffin know what she wanted. After their romantic dinner at the Celeste Restaurant, Griffin and Taylor ended up back at her place where she lived with her parents. Griffin couldn't resist her sweet, passionate kisses, her vivacious personality, and the tender touch of her fingertips. Griffin and Taylor spent the night making passionate love in her bed. They both knew it would be their last night spent together for a very long time. It was one of the most difficult decisions Griffin ever had to make. He would head out early Thursday morning for his first sixty-city book tour and would be gone for six months. The only way Griffin and Taylor would be able to see each other would be through Facetime or Skype video chats, texts, or phone calls.

Taylor and Griffin had known each other and dated for almost a year. They had been through some difficult times together with the motorcycle accident, hospital stays, and surgeries. Their love had grown strong, and they were inseparable. Yet, Griffin and Taylor would have to maintain a long-distance relationship if they were going to make it work between the two of them. It would require much patience and sacrifice on both of their parts. Even though Taylor wanted to be a groupie and Griffin's *girlfriend* throughout his book tour, it would be difficult, if not impossible. Sheldon House had made it very clear Griffin's tour was, "strictly business"—no partying, no drinking, no sex, no drugs, and no girls. Also, if Taylor toured with him, no one would offer to pay for her food, travel, and personal expenses. And even though Griffin had made those points clear to Taylor as to why she couldn't tour with him, something told him he might see her again during his tour. She might show up somewhere on the road when he least expected it.

Taylor took the separation hard, but so did Griffin. All the adventures and hard times with Taylor had to be shelved for now. When Griffin told her the news a few weeks ago, her face had turned fiery red. She couldn't accept it. She folded her tense arms, stood her ground in protest, and shouted four-letter words at him. That was after she tried to sweeten him up with every promise in the world. She begged, pleaded with him, and then when Griffin wouldn't budge, she turned her back, took large, heavy steps in protest, and kept her distance from him so she could have a good crying party.

Griffin's first tour city outside of Chicago was Madison, Wisconsin. He wasn't familiar with Madison as he hadn't been outside of Chicago except for the time he flew to New York City to meet with Mr. Turnbull.

Mr. Turnbull and Sheldon House decided to transport Griffin around on his tour by train or airplane. They decided for him to travel by train to Madison. Griffin had to wake up early on Wednesday morning to catch the 6:10 a.m. Amtrak train from downtown Chicago to Madison.

Griffin packed his clothes, toiletries, and a few books and headed toward the train station with his mom. She graciously volunteered to make the sacrifice of waking up at five a.m. to fix him breakfast and take him to the station. She wanted to send Griffin off with her special hugs and kisses. It was sentimental to her. She wouldn't see her son for at least six months, so she wanted to make the final moment she'd see him special. Griffin's dad was a whole different beast. He needed his sleep for work, so he couldn't be bothered with driving Griffin to the train station.

When they arrived, Griffin's mom parked her car and followed him through the crowded waiting area to the terminal where he would board. Griffin could tell that even though she was proud of him, she didn't want to let him go.

This is going to be a tough moment for her. She could lose it; she could fall apart right here in the train station, Griffin thought.

The minute Griffin had to board, she held onto him like a frightened child in a department store who had just been found in a Code Adam. Her arms surrounded his entire body with her face buried into his chest. Suddenly, Griffin was her lifeline. She was sobbing as her faced became entirely water-soaked and chafed. It was a hard thing to do—to let her go and for her to let Griffin go.

Griffin took his seat by the window in the crowded train. The train pulled away from the station at precisely 6:10 a.m. as he waved goodbye. He acted like he was some *manly man* who didn't cry, but he found himself choking up with intense tears as they streamed down his face.

Griffin was headed for Madison. It was a bittersweet day for him. He was experiencing high anxiety over his first, out-of-town book signing, unsure of what to expect, and he was sad that he wouldn't see his mom for at least six months.

***

When I wrote this chapter, I felt like the bad guy for leaving Taylor back in Chicago as I started my book tour. I wasn't sure if Taylor would ever speak to me again.

CHAPTER THIRTY-FOUR
HIGH ANXIETY

What if no one shows for my book signing? What if I don't sell any books? Griffin thought.

The questions haunted Griffin like other annoying regrets from the past. This was to be the first signing outside of his hometown. No one would know him like they'd known their "hometown boy." This would be the first major test of whether Griffin could draw crowds and sell books.

What if the tour flopped and Griffin was a big disappointment for Mr. Turnbull and Sheldon House? They had sunk a lot of money into him, and it would be a catastrophe if he let them down. Before Griffin could worry any further, he watched the train pull up to the Columbus, Wisconsin Amtrak Station. It was nothing spectacular. It was an interesting-looking stone building with the words Columbus carved into the stone directly above the large, white-trimmed windows. Below the large windows were window boxes filled with plastic tulips and daffodils. There were three doors: a bright red one, a dark blue one, and a brown one. The sky was clouded with gray. As Griffin put one foot off the train and touched the pavement, he felt a chilly wind blow through him. Before Griffin could enter the building, his eyes spotted a rather tall man dressed in a gray sports coat, dress pants, and a striped red and blue necktie. The man wore a gray dress hat, stylish black-rimmed glasses, and a khaki London Fog overcoat. He resembled a spy working for some foreign government. He appeared to be about fiftyish. His body was leaning against the stone building, trying to keep warm from the chilly wind. He held a three-foot, cardboard sign with the letters of Griffin's first and last names in bright red.

He also held a copy of Griffin's new book. There was no way Griffin would ever miss him. Griffin took a few steps to where the man was standing and reached out to shake his hand.

"Hi, I'm Griffin Smith."

The man must have been preoccupied, daydreaming, or ignoring Griffin for the moment because it seemed like Griffin had caught him off guard. The man reached out to shake Griffin's hand.

"I'm Robert Thurgood, III. I'll be your author escort while you're here in Madison."

"Excellent," Griffin said.

"I'll take your bag. My car's parked over there," Mr. Thurgood said.

It was one of those black Tahoes that government officials drive. Griffin wondered if he had been hired by Sheldon House or if the man worked for the U.S. Government. He didn't quite fit the part of an author escort, but what did Griffin know?

Mr. Thurgood unlocked his Tahoe and threw Griffin's bag into the back seat as Griffin seated himself in the beige, leather front seat and locked his seatbelt into place. Mr. Thurgood started the engine, and they took off to a destination unknown.

"I guess you know Madison is about thirty miles from here. Amtrak doesn't have a station in the city, so we have to drive out of our way to catch the train," Mr. Thurgood said.

"That's good to know," Griffin said.

"I read your debut book, and it is very good for a kid your age. How old did you say you are?" Mr. Thurgood asked.

"Nineteen," Griffin replied.

"That means you probably wrote the book when you were seventeen or eighteen, and you just turned nineteen," Mr. Thurgood said.

"You've got it," Griffin replied.

Mr. Thurgood rarely smiled, and he spoke with a dry sense of humor. You had to get to know him before making a judgment about him. Griffin would decide how he felt about Thurgood in due time—perhaps by the end of the day.

"You have two radio interviews today, three radio shows and two television appearances tomorrow, some interviews with *The Badger Herald, The Capital Times, Wisconsin State Journal,* and *Action 2 News* on Friday." Thurgood said.

"Wow, that's a lot to keep track of," Griffin said.

"That's why you've got me to keep you on track," Mr. Thurgood replied.

He's either a wise guy or slightly conceited, Griffin thought.

"This is the exit we take to your hotel," Mr. Thurgood said.

It was awkwardly silent, except for the humming of the car engine.

"Here we are, 525 West Johnson Street. This Doubletree Hotel is first class," Mr. Thurgood said.

Mr. Thurgood pulled the Tahoe up to the hotel front door, left the engine running, and helped Griffin with his bag. He opened the large glass door and led Griffin to the front counter. Thurgood dropped his ID and company credit card down on the counter.

"This is Griffin Smith. He will be staying with you from today through Sunday. Give him the best room you've got," Mr. Thurgood said.

"Why sure," the hotel clerk said.

They both stood without saying a word to each other in the hotel lobby as the background music played. The clerk was swiping the credit card and logging information for Griffin's stay.

"I'll need to see Mr. Smith's ID," the clerk said.

Griffin handed it to her.

A few minutes of silence passed.

"Here's your ID back. Just sign here," the clerk said.

He scribbled his, Griffin Smith, at the bottom of the printed form.

"Okay, you can take it from here. You're an adult now and you know what to do."

"Thanks, Mr. Thurgood." Griffin said.

"Don't thank me, thank Sheldon House. I'll stop tomorrow at five a.m.," Thurgood said.

They both paused in silence.

Did he say five a.m.? Griffin thought.

Griffin's face looked completely puzzled.

"Yes, you heard me right, five a.m. tomorrow morning. We've got a whole slew of early morning radio shows to cover," Thurgood said.

As Griffin walked toward his room, he got an unexpected text on his phone from Taylor.

Hiiiii   I misssssss YOU.

Griffin knew it could be a long night.

***

Taylor's surprise text message made me wonder if Taylor would try to make our long-distance relationship work. She was persistent with her messages. It also made me wonder if she might show up unannounced in one of the cities on my schedule.

CHAPTER THIRTY-FIVE
A ROOM OF ONE'S OWN

If someone had told Griffin a day with Mr. Thurgood would be fun, he would've said they were lying. But the next couple days turned out to be a whole lot of fun. Griffin was beginning to understand Mr. Thurgood's dry sense of humor, and Thurgood was starting to understand Griffin.

Griffin lived up to his end of the bargain, and Thurgood kept his word too. Thurgood was a cross between the fun dad Griffin wished he could've had and a fun uncle Griffin never knew. Just when he thought Mr. Thurgood was getting way too serious, he would say something so funny that it made Griffin roll on the floor with non-stop laughter.

Griffin and Thurgood humored each other through the next couple of days with the radio, television, newspaper interviews, and guest appearances. Through it all, Mr. Thurgood always found something funny to say. He'd lighten up the interviews with in-between visits to the park, ice cream stores, the video arcade, and games of laser tag. What kid wouldn't like that?

The rest of the week flew by way too fast. On Saturday, they arrived at one p.m. at the bookstore called A Room of One's Own. Griffin's book signing event was supposed to start at two p.m. The bookstore was like no bookstore Griffin had seen before. A large, burgundy, half-circle awning with the logo and name of the bookstore printed in white hung in front of the store. The outside of the bookstore was brick with large display windows. At the top of the awning and windows, directly above the front doors, was a shelf of colorful books and large eloquent white bold lettering that read from left to right: BOOKS NEW AND USED----A ROOM OF ONE'S

OWN BOOKSTORE. Six old-looking, gooseneck lamps were positioned outside above the banner. Griffin and Thurgood entered the large double doors, and, to their surprise, what appeared to be a small mom and pop store, was open and spacious on the inside. The large, open space in the center of the store was covered with an attractive light-brown carpet. And to the right and left, spacious rooms filled with numerous books of all shapes and sizes on tall oak shelves welcomed readers. The walls were painted a sun-colored yellow with white mold trimming all around the ceiling. A friendly, welcoming ambiance could be felt by customers when they stepped inside the store.

The owners, Sal Ellis and Teresa Goodall, beamed with radiant smiles. They could strike up a conversation about almost anything. They treated Griffin and Thurgood like VIPs and were grateful that Sheldon House had chosen their store to host one of Griffin's book signing events. Sal and Teresa were eager to help them set up chairs, tables, and the podium. They even had a small P.A. system with a wireless mic to use when Griffin spoke. He was impressed with them and the way they managed their store. They had life-size posters of Griffin and his book in display windows, and they had free-standing life-size posters of Griffin displayed throughout the various rooms. Mr. Thurgood took some photos of Griffin beside one of the life-size posters. He got a few photos of Sal, Teresa, and him before the event started.

"We put out one hundred chairs, and we've got more if we need them," Sal said.

"Yep, and we've advertised this for weeks on radio, television, and social media," Teresa added.

"Awesome," Griffin said.

"You should have a good crowd today," Mr. Thurgood said.

"We've got the table covered with your books. We will assist you in the signing process," Sal said.

"Anything I need to know before we begin?" Griffin asked.

"Yes, we will form a line with the cash register positioned at the beginning of the line," Teresa said.

"As we sell each book, Mr. Thurgood will hand it to you to sign," Sal said.

"Good, I can't wait," Griffin said.

"Look, they're already starting to come in," Mr. Thurgood whispered to Griffin.

Thurgood was right. A large crowd of all ages and sizes poured in. Men, women, teens, and children quickly took their seats. It was about one fifty p.m. and the crowd kept pouring in. Sal and Teresa realized they needed to set up more chairs. They put out an extra seventy-five chairs and all were filled. They ran out of chairs, which was a good problem to have, but the crowd kept pouring in. Suddenly a relatively quiet bookstore became noisy with laughter and chatter.

It was only three minutes before show time with a shoulder-to-shoulder, standing-room-only crowd. The room became stuffy and hot from all the people trying to catch Griffin's book event.

"We've reached our capacity. What are we going to do?" Sal asked.

"If someone reports us, the Fire Marshal could shut us down," Teresa said.

"We can't turn them away. We have to give them what we advertised," Sal said.

"I guess we'll take our chances," Teresa replied.

"Let's get started; it's a few minutes after two," Mr. Thurgood said.

Griffin's stomach churned excessively. He thought he might have to make a run for the bathroom, but he took a few, deep breaths and let them out slowly. He pulled himself together.

"You can do this, Griffin, " he told himself.

Mr. Thurgood introduced Griffin to the crowd.

Griffin took a few reluctant steps toward the podium. A sea of faces covered every inch of the building. The audience was pressed shoulder-to-shoulder against each wall. People were lined up outside the door waiting to get in. There could've easily been three hundred people inside and waiting outside the bookstore.

As Griffin reached the podium, the crowd gave him a loud, resounding chorus of cheers and applause.

"Griffin, Griffin," they chanted.

It was almost cultish the way the crowd greeted him.

Griffin stood in front of all those faces and smiled without saying a word until the crowd quieted down.

"Wow, I love you too, Madison," were Griffin's first words.

The crowd started chanting and cheering again. He felt like he was inside a political rally where he was their favorite candidate.

Again, Griffin waited until the crowd finished chanting. A few minutes later, the decibels dropped to almost nil.

"This is so overwhelming, particularly for a nineteen-year-old," Griffin said. His voice broke as he choked up with tears.

"Griffin, Griffin, Griffin," the crowd continued chanting.

Griffin was so new at book-signing events that he wasn't sure how to quiet the noisy crowd. So, he waited without saying a word and smiled through it all.

Finally, Griffin was able to tell them about his book, and he read one of his favorite chapters. Griffin told them how honored he was to be in their presence. He told them how much he enjoyed the book and how much it meant for him to read it to them.

Forty-five minutes later with a gazillion questions answered, Griffin's book presentation ended with thunderous applause and the crowd giving him a standing, cheering ovation. Mr. Thurgood, Sal, and Theresa surrounded him. They escorted Griffin to the front of the store where the cash register and a spread of books rested on the tables. Flocks of people rushed to Griffin, trying to touch him and get selfies with him. Griffin managed to make it to the tables at the front of the store with the assistance of Sal, Teresa, and Mr. Thurgood.

A long, single-file line of people formed. The line was organized with ropes and resembled the curvy, parallel lines you would see at Disneyland. The line overwhelmingly continued throughout the store, outside the store, and spilled onto the sidewalk beside the street

"It's good it's not a rainy day or all these people would not be standing outside waiting," Mr. Thurgood said.

Griffin met Paul, Cheyenne, Abby, Eddy, Louis, and Taylor. The faces and names went on and on. He greeted everyone with a smile and a selfie. Griffin signed every book with a personal message.

God, my hand and arm are getting sore, Griffin thought.

He must have signed over two hundred and fifty of his books. Not only were his hand and arms suffering from writer's cramps, but his legs were starting to give in to fatigue.

Griffin looked up while signing a book, and it appeared the line hadn't diminished.

"Griffin, we've only got three more of your books left," Mr. Thurgood said.

"What do you want to do?" Griffin asked.

"We can take orders and get the books to them ASAP," Sal said.

The moment the crowd heard there were only three books left, they started pushing and shoving in line to get the last three copies.

Griffin smiled and signed the last three copies.

"I am so sorry that we ran out of books," he said.

"How soon can we get a copy?" a man asked.

"Yeah, I want a copy now," a woman said.

"We're truly sorry that we ran out of books. If you would please write your name and contact information on this form, I will personally make sure you get a copy as soon as I get one in my hands," Sal told the disappointed crowd.

Nevertheless, the crowd in line stayed and requested Griffin's autograph on anything they could find—receipts, bank deposit slips, and random pieces of paper. He obliged until everyone in line had greeted him. Even though the ones who didn't get books were disappointed, they placed orders with Sal and Teresa.

Finally, it was quiet. Everyone had left. Griffin had a chance to check his phone. The clock said it was six p.m.

"How could it be six p.m.?" Griffin asked.

"It's been a long day. We've been here for five hours including set-up time," Mr. Thurgood said.

"You and your book were a hit," Sal said.

"Thanks, I had a lot of fun." Griffin replied.

171

Silence overcame him as he yawned.

"Too bad we ran out of books," Griffin said.

"Don't feel too bad. We sold out of all your books," Sal said.

"Yep, we ordered two hundred and seventy-five copies and sold every one," Teresa added.

Sal and Teresa were proudly beaming at their accomplishment.

"And we've got orders for one hundred and fifty more copies," Sal said.

"That was nothing short of a miracle, Griffin," Teresa said.

"This is a record for us in book sales," Sal agreed.

"We'd like to have you back, Griffin," Teresa said.

"Thanks," Griffin replied.

"I'm sure Sheldon House could arrange that. We'll take you up on that offer," Mr. Thurgood said.

"Please do," Sal added.

"Thank you, Sal and Theresa, for hosting my book signing event," Griffin said.

He reached out to shake their hands, but they threw their arms around him with hugs

"Well, this about wraps up all I was hired to do," Mr. Thurgood said.

"Thanks, Mr. Thurgood. I appreciate all you've done. You're a terrific author escort."

"I'm getting tired and heading back home. Here's one hundred dollars for you to get an Uber, get some dinner, and spend a night on the town. You know where your hotel is, and you seem like a responsible adult. So, I'm going to let you have some time to yourself. Go have fun. You deserve it," Thurgood said.

"Thanks, Mr. Thurgood," Griffin said.

"I'll pick you up in the morning about eleven a.m. and take you to the Amtrak station so you can be on your way to the next town," Mr. Thurgood said.

Griffin shook his hand and waved goodbye as Thurgood started up his Tahoe to head home. He rolled down the window as he drove his car past Griffin.

"Don't do anything I wouldn't do, kid," Thurgood said.

As much as Griffin liked Thurgood, he was unaware that Thurgood was reporting every little detail back to Turnbull as Turnbull had hired him to do. Turnbull had to make sure everything was accurate on Griffin in the book Turnbull was writing.

Everything was almost perfect for Griffin today. There was only one thing missing, Taylor. His day would have been perfect with her by his side.

CHAPTER THIRTY-SIX
ALL OVER THE MAP

Griffin hated to see Mr. Thurgood go. He was a very entertaining man. Griffin's first impressions of Thurgood left much to be desired. But he was a damn good author escort.

"If all the escorts are as good as him, I'll be in good shape on this tour," he told himself.

Mr. Thurgood was such a detailed and thorough man. He was very punctual and was just what Griffin needed for his Madison tour. Thurgood arrived at Griffin's hotel ten minutes before the eleven a.m. scheduled time and got Griffin to the Columbus Amtrak station well before his noon departure.

The next six weeks were nothing but a whirlwind, city-to-city, fast-paced tour. The next stop was Des Moines, Iowa, then Saint Paul, Minnesota, and then off to Fargo, North Dakota—all courtesy of Amtrak and Sheldon House. Griffin could hardly catch his breath or get a break. The sad part about the whole drill was Griffin lost touch with Taylor. They didn't text, talk, or video chat anymore. It had been weeks since he had heard from her. It made Griffin sad.

It was the same ole drill from week to week. Griffin practically had his schedule memorized. He'd meet the author escort assigned to each city at the train station, and he or she would pick him up and drive him to his hotel. Griffin would do a gazillion radio, television, and newspaper interviews, and he'd usually hold his book signing event on a Saturday afternoon. His schedule was like clockwork; everything ran together.

Apparently, the rigid touring from city-to-city was working. Week after week, Griffin received personal calls from Mr. Turnbull praising him on his appearances and boasting about how many books they had sold. Every time he'd call, Mr. Turnbull told Griffin he was the master of Griffin's destiny. Turnbull said he could make anything happen for him. It was creepy and weird, but Griffin figured Turnbull knew what he was doing.

The cities and towns all started to look alike, except for the weather. The weather could be sunny one day, cloudy the next, and rainy or snowy on another day.

Griffin was homesick. He called his mom and dad frequently as he traveled from city to city. He tried to connect with Taylor, but she was either too busy or perhaps, she was done with him.

God, I hate to admit this, but I miss them, Griffin thought.

Griffin lost track of all the book signings and radio/television interviews he had done. He must've met thousands of people so far. Trouble is, he couldn't remember any of their names.

One day, after Griffin had traveled to Sioux City, South Dakota; Rapid City, South Dakota; and Denver, Colorado, he received an urgent call from Mr. Turnbull.

"Griffin, are you sitting down?" Turnbull asked.

Griffin was totally caught by surprise. He held onto his end of the phone with a tight, nervous grip wondering what Mr. Turnbull would tell him.

"Yes, I'm sitting down," Griffin replied.

"Your book is in the top ten of the *New York Times* bestsellers list," Turnbull said.

A long pause of silence lingered between them

"Did you hear me, Griffin? I said your book is in the top ten," Turnbull said.

"I heard you loud and clear," Griffin replied.

"I'm emailing you a copy of the *New York Times* list," Turnbull said.

"Awesome," Griffin replied.

Griffin jumped up and down with excitement to hear the news. It had been his lifelong dream to make it into the *New York Times* bestsellers list.

"You better believe it's awesome, Griffin. That is a record for a nineteen-year-old author. I am the reason you are where you are today," Turnbull said.

"Of course, you are, you're my publisher," Griffin replied.

"No, I mean I've fixed things so that they happen the way they were meant to be," Turnbull said.

"What do you mean you fixed things?" Griffin asked.

The words between them fell silent. Turnbull was scaring Griffin with his comments. Griffin wasn't sure what Turnbull meant by him being the master of Griffin's destiny. He was afraid to pry further perhaps knowing he might learn more than he'd care to know.

Mr. Turnbull's words are creepy. He's going a little too far to suggest he can control my life, Griffin thought.

"Mr. Turnbull, I respect you. I appreciate all you've done to promote my new book. But I can make many decisions on my own. No one is in control of me. I am in control of myself," Griffin said.

Mr. Turnbull roared with laughter which almost seemed evil-sounding.

"You just think you are, son," Turnbull said.

Griffin was not ready to argue with Mr. Turnbull today, so he changed the subject.

"How many books do you think I've sold so far?" Griffin asked.

"I can give you a rough estimate. Hold on a minute and I'll tell you," Turnbull said.

The silence and suspense were killing Griffin while waiting for Mr. Turnbull to tell him the numbers.

"I'm back, Griffin. The Nielson Book Scan and Amazon sales are about 1,557,952 copies sold."

"Seriously?" Griffin asked.

"Yes, seriously. That's extraordinary for a debut author. By my projection, we should reach two million sometime after Christmas," Turnbull said.

"Really?" Griffin said.

Griffin lunged his tightly closed fist with his arm toward the ceiling expressing his excitement and joy.

176

"Yes, really. It's time to start thinking about a follow-up book to *A Novel Life*," Turnbull said.

"A follow-up book, huh?" Griffin asked.

"Yes, Griffin, a follow-up book. Do you have any great ideas?" Turnbull asked.

Griffin scratched his head thinking about any ideas that came to mind.

"I'll think about it," Griffin replied.

Suddenly, Mr. Turnbull burst out laughing.

"You'll think about it? Don't think about it but start getting busy working on it," Turnbull commanded.

Mr. Turnbull was ordering Griffin around as if he owned him. Suddenly, Griffin realized he hadn't signed up for such pressure and all the stress that came with it.

"No worries, Mr. Turnbull; I'll get on it right away," Griffin said.

Griffin told Turnbull the words he wanted to hear so he could get him off his back. It worked for the time being.

"Good answer, Griffin," he said. "I will talk to you soon."

Turnbull hung up. Griffin took a long, deep breath and exhaled. For the moment, Griffin got Turnbull off his back. But he wasn't out of the woods yet.

CHAPTER THIRTY-SEVEN
TODAY OF ALL DAYS

It was totally unexpected. Griffin was caught off guard. It was as if the universe had shifted and all the planets had conveniently lined up perfectly in Griffin's favor. It happened, today of all days.

Griffin was deep into his tour, having completed twenty-six book signings, forty-two radio interviews, thirty-two television appearances, and twenty-seven newspaper interviews. At every stop along the way, Griffin had large enthusiastic crowds of fans, many shouting his name, rushing and pushing through the long lines to meet him. Most wanted selfies and his, "Griffin Smith," scribbled across their books. He had massive crowds.

Today was different. It was the second Saturday of January. Griffin was in Laramie, Wyoming, population 32,473. The clouds had covered what little sunshine was left. It was an unusually warm day as compared to the January Chicago weather Griffin was used to. The weather forecasters had predicted the next five days to have the daytime high of sixty-four degrees with a low at nights of fifty-five.

Sheldon House had arranged for Griffin to hook up with his author escort in Laramie. Her name was Elsie Freemyer. She was fifty-nine years of age, petite in size, had gray bee-hive hair, and wore black, horn-rimmed glasses with a silver chain attached to her neck. She reminded Griffin of the old-school librarian he had back at Lincoln Elementary. She was prim and proper. Elsie wore a pale, beige and pink pant suit with a bright floral-colored blouse. She greeted him with his book in hand on Thursday at Laramie Regional Airport. Elsie was a motherly type to Griffin—always keeping him on schedule with his days and evenings filled with radio, television, and newspaper interviews. Elsie carried the company credit card and paid for all Griffin's meals, transportation, and hotel expenses while staying in Laramie.

The owner of Second Story Bookstore had promised a good crowd for Griffin at the two p.m. time slot. The cute, red brick independent bookstore with a long, bright, blue-and-white striped awning was frequented by almost everyone in town. Who wouldn't have wanted to visit this charming bookstore? It also had a used bookstore and a quaint-looking café next door, called the Night Heron.

The clock read 1:30 p.m. Elsie helped set up the chairs, podium, and posters and neatly arranged a nice spread of Griffin's books on the tables for eagerly awaiting fans seeking his autograph. The store owner was expecting a crowd of well over one hundred and twenty-five. It would be an, "overflow," crowd. Griffin's event was advertised on radio, television, social media, and in newspapers that covered a radius of at least a hundred miles and beyond.

Blame it on a cloudy day, blame it on the unusually warm Saturday date, blame it on whatever, but two o'clock came and there were only six people in the audience. That was counting the store owner, Elsie, and four strangers to make it a grand total of a whopping six people. It was humbling and brought Griffin's mile-high ego down to five-feet-eight inches. But Mr. Turnbull had always told Griffin to give his best performance whether he had a crowd of a thousand or only three—the show must go on.

"Here goes nothing," Griffin told himself.

Griffin stood behind the podium and tried to put on his best smile for the underwhelmed, puny audience. Little did he know, only an hour from now, the humiliation of being cut down to size would be long forgotten. Elsie introduced him and took a seat as Griffin began his presentation.

This is awkward. I feel like I'm talking to myself, Griffin thought.

"Hi, I'm Griffin Smith, author of *A Novel Life*. I am honored to share my life story with you."

The room grew still with a mad deafening silence.

"I guess they didn't get the memo," he said.

Suddenly the silence was broken. All six people were laughing, including Elsie.

Griffin took a deep breath and continued. He was feeling more at ease. Finally, Griffin had the tiny audience on his side. Griffin told stories from his heart; stories people could relate to. The whole event didn't last for more than thirty minutes, counting the four books he signed.

I can't believe I only sold four books, Griffin thought.

Griffin thanked the store owner for her time in scheduling the event. The moment felt awkward trying to force a confident, pleasant smile, knowing how small the crowd was. Yet Elsie and Griffin became Oscar Award-winning actors that day for their roles, putting on the best faces despite all the odds against them.

As Elsie and Griffin opened the large wooden door of the bookstore, Griffin's body accidentally slammed into someone who was rushing to enter the building. Griffin had his head down, with his eyes buried in his phone, as he checked his messages. Elsie tried to warn him.

"Watch out, Griffin," she said.

But it was too late. Two bodies collided. As Griffin's head rose to an upright position, his eyes slowly caught sight of a beautiful, familiar face. Griffin was completely thrown off guard by the surprise.

"Taylor, my God, it's you, " Griffin said.

Griffin's eyes stared at her radiant beauty. Taylor wore a stunning short red dress with her hair up in a bun and a decorative, butterfly hairpiece. Griffin reached out to hug her. His lips touched Taylor's as they kissed affectionately while they held each other in a passionate embrace.

"God, I've missed you," Taylor said.

"Me too," Griffin answered.

"I'm sorry, Griffin, for running into you like that," Taylor said as she giggled.

"No worries, I'm so happy to see you," Griffin replied.

"Please accept our apologies for not paying attention while we were walking," Elsie said.

"No, it was my fault. I was in a hurry, trying to catch Griffin's book signing," Taylor said.

"I'm sorry to say my author event ended about ten minutes ago," Griffin replied.

"Oh, my gosh, I can't believe it. I thought it was at three," Taylor said. "I'm so sorry I missed your book signing, Griffin."

"It was at two p.m. today," Elsie said.

"Damn, I really wanted to see you speak, Griffin," Taylor sighed.

Taylor continued to rub her face with her right index finger in a nervous manner. Her face looked flushed, red with embarrassment and nervousness.

"No need to worry, Taylor. I am so glad you are here," Griffin said. "Perhaps I can give you a private reading of my book."

Taylor batted her eyelids, and her face lit up with an enormous smile.

"I would love that, Griffin," Taylor replied.

Griffin returned the smile with a radiant, giddy look on his face.

"Oh, by the way, this is Elsie Freemyer, my author escort."

"So glad to meet you, Ms. Freemyer," Taylor said.

"Pleased to meet you too, Taylor," Elise answered.

It had been almost four months since Griffin had seen Taylor face-to-face. Griffin had photos of her on his phone and remembered in his mind how gorgeous Taylor was. But this time Griffin saw Taylor in a different light. Griffin saw new, attractive features and qualities in Taylor he hadn't noticed before. Taylor's emerald green eyes sparkled brighter than Griffin had ever seen them. Her long brown locks captivated Griffin like nothing he'd ever seen. Taylor's facial complexion was smooth and silky, a pinkish white color, with a perfectly shaped face. Her cheeks were tastefully sprinkled with freckles. Why hadn't he noticed these stunning attributes in Taylor before? Taylor had soft, voluptuous red lips. When she smiled, she revealed enticing dimples that couldn't be ignored. At the moment, Griffin couldn't think of anything else but Taylor. His eyes couldn't help but stare at Taylor, admiring her beauty. He felt drawn to Taylor like a magnet attracts shiny metal. Griffin was speechless because she was so breathtaking.

I don't think you could be any more obvious, Griffin, he thought.

Taylor giggled with giddy laughter as her face blushed.

"Taylor, you've always been the most beautiful woman in the world to me, but this time you're absolutely stunning."

Taylor grinned and giggled with silly laughter.

"Aw, Griffin, you're so sweet, thank you."

Taylor rushed into Griffin's arms and gave him the sweetest kiss. They held each other in a tight embrace for a moment. Then Griffin took Taylor's hand and asked her if she'd like to take a walk.

"Sure," Taylor answered.

Griffin and Taylor took a few slow steps down the sidewalk with his hand in hers and stopped.

"How's your mom and dad?" Griffin asked.

"Well, Dad is worried about losing his job, and Mom is wrapped up in her work," Taylor replied.

"I'm sorry to hear about your dad. How's your sister?" Griffin asked.

"She's still a brat like she's always been," Taylor answered.

Griffin burst out laughing at Taylor's unexpected reply.

"So, Taylor, what have you been up to lately?" Griffin asked.

"I can't decide what to do with my life," Taylor replied. "I've decided to take some time off before I go to college."

"Well, you've always been good at science. Maybe you could do something in the medical field," Griffin said.

"Nah, don't think so," Taylor replied.

"And you've always loved English. You could be an author," Griffin said.

"Do you really think so?" Taylor asked.

"Of course. You can do anything, Taylor," Griffin replied.

"It's funny you mentioned being an author," Taylor said. "I've written some short stories and a novel I'd like you to see since you are a big-time, famous author."

"Sure, anytime. I'd love to read them," Griffin said.

Elsie watched the intense, chemical attraction between Taylor and Griffin. They left Elsie completely out of the conversation, standing all by herself. She was still in their sight, only a few feet away. Taylor and Griffin had tuned her out and rudely left her standing all alone. Elsie fidgeted and paced in circles. She eventually walked up to Taylor and Griffin, interrupting them.

"I don't mean to butt in. I'm heading home because it's been a long day. Griffin, you know where the hotel is. You have enough cash for dinner and an Uber. I'll call you in the morning about our plans for the week," Elsie said.

"Okay, Elsie. Thank you for your help today. You did a great job," Griffin replied.

"Don't mention it. Go and have a good time. See you soon," Elsie said. She looked like she wanted to wring Griffin's neck.

"Taylor, would you like to get dinner with me at the café next door?" Griffin asked.

"Sure, I'd love to," Taylor replied.

Taylor's face illuminated like a million stars lighting up the night. Griffin didn't know where their conversation would lead to, but he imagined where he wanted it to go. He was entranced.

Taylor was an amazing woman. She was like every woman in the world all built into one woman. Even her mannerisms and the charismatic way words rolled off her tongue mesmerized Griffin.

Something's drastically wrong with this picture. I can't figure it out, Griffin thought.

It was as if Griffin had lived this life before. It was hauntingly familiar—the town, the people, the buildings, the streets, and even the surprise visit by Taylor. He had never set foot into the town of Laramie. In fact, he'd never even heard of the town until now.

Impossible, Griffin thought.

Griffin knew this wasn't a dream or a figment of his imagination. He knew he wasn't dead because Griffin could feel, touch, see, taste, and breathe all his surroundings. He was perplexed. It was a mystery that haunted him, and he had to solve that mystery.

Griffin and Taylor walked together, hand-in-hand toward the Night Heron. He opened the door for her. They found a cozy table in the corner for two. Taylor's whole life, the part Griffin never knew, would unfold right before Griffin's eyes. Griffin and Taylor talked, laughed, and cried together until the Night Heron manager asked them to leave as they were the last ones lingering around and keeping the café from closing. Even though it was forbidden by Turnbull and Elsie, Griffin invited Taylor to spend the night with him in his hotel room. She accepted his invitation, and they kept their hotel rendezvous a secret.

***

This chapter represents one of my most memorable moments. I considered it a turning point in my life when Taylor showed up at my poorly-attended book signing event. The event was a blessing in disguise, because of the, "meant-to-be," moment when Taylor entered my life again. She suddenly changed everything.

CHAPTER THIRTY-EIGHT
INSEPARABLE

The next morning, Griffin and Taylor woke up in each other's arms, cheek to cheek, with giddy smiles on their faces. Griffin passionately kissed Taylor's lips, and she returned his tender gesture. They held their naked bodies closer than paper stuck together with glue. Griffin and Taylor became quickly enamored with each other again and felt the burning urge to make love for the umpteenth time. The two of them took a break, gasped for oxygen, and laid next to each other with pleasant, relaxed faces. Griffin gently brushed Taylor's face as he whispered to her.

"Amazing, Taylor, you are simply amazing."

"You, too, Griffin," Taylor replied.

Griffin smiled and kissed her on the lips. Then Griffin reached for his cell phone and checked his messages.

"God, it's already eleven a.m., and Elsie hasn't called," Griffin said. "I thought she might have called our room."

"Maybe, you should check with the front desk," Taylor suggested.

Griffin checked with the front desk on the hotel phone. Elsie hadn't called or left any messages. Griffin thought about what day it was and if he had any book signings or radio/TV interviews.

"Now I remember Elise saying I had the day off today, no events," Griffin said.

"That's good for us," Taylor replied.

Taylor rolled her naked body over from her front to her side and winked at Griffin as she kissed his lips. He pulled her in closer and kissed her.

"Do you want to get some lunch?" Griffin asked.

"Sure," Taylor replied.

Griffin and Taylor rolled out of bed and waited for the other to shower and get dressed.

"Since, we're trying to keep our sleeping together a secret, we should leave the room separately," Taylor suggested.

"Agreed," Griffin replied.

Griffin and Taylor each left the hotel room alone about five minutes apart from the other. They met in the parking lot and they stepped inside an Uber they had requested earlier. Griffin and Taylor headed to a cozy, romantic café they had seen online, called Jeffrey's Bistro located on East Iverson Street. When they arrived, the hostess seated them at a corner table in the back away from the crowd. Griffin and Taylor admired the solid cherry tables and chairs mixed with the interior brick walls and wide-planked wooden floors. Their eyes caught the perfect décor of old knick-knack objects and wall hangings accenting the dimmed lights. They loved the atmosphere, the aroma of gourmet food cooking, and the hint of soft music playing in the background. Soon, the waiter greeted them and took their orders. Now they were free to talk about whatever until lunch arrived.

Taylor and Griffin exchanged giddy smiles with each other. Taylor twirled her hair and batted her eyes. Griffin's face was flushed from his intense feelings for her.

"Tell me about this dream of yours to write," Griffin asked.

"I love to write. I took several English classes at William Fentress High and made As. Mom and Dad want me to get a real job like teaching English at a high school," Taylor said.

"But what do you want to do?" Griffin asked.

"I'd love to be a successful author like you," Taylor said.

Griffin paused for a few seconds to think about what Taylor had said. He couldn't hide the flustered look on his face. His face revealed his true colors. It was fully flushed with a silly-looking, yet confident grin.

"That's kind of you to say, Taylor," Griffin said.

"I mean it," Taylor replied.

"What kind of author do you want to be?" Griffin asked.

"A number-one bestselling fiction author," Taylor responded.

Wow, that's confidence, Griffin thought.

"It's a lot of hard work; but if anyone can do it, you can," Griffin said.

Taylor smiled from cheek-to-cheek and her beauty beamed radiantly. She rose from her chair and reached her arms toward Griffin. Taylor gave him a tight, warm and lengthy hug. He could feel the softness of her hair and arms as they brushed against his hands. Taylor's scent was inviting. Griffin swore she was wearing his favorite gardenia-scented perfume. Taylor's arms were a soft and gentle place to be. Griffin didn't want to let go of them or her, but she released her arms as her eyes stared with a glazed look straight into his. She believed in Griffin.

"Aww, that's the kindest thing anyone has ever said to me." Taylor said.

"Well, it's true," Griffin replied.

"No one in my family believes in my writing abilities. They don't take me seriously," Taylor said."

"That's sad. I'd like to see some of your work. I bet I'd believe in your writing if I were able to read some of it," Griffin said in a flirting manner.

"Thank you, Griffin. I've never really shown it to anyone before," Taylor said.

"You can show it to me anytime," Griffin said.

"You mean it?" Taylor asked.

"Yes, most definitely," Griffin replied.

Taylor's face lit up like a million stars illuminating the night.

"Seriously though, what kind of genres do you write?" Griffin asked.

"I've got some short stories written, but I've been working on my novel for some time now," she replied.

"What's it about?" he asked.

"It's a romance novel about a boy and girl who come from completely different backgrounds and yet they make it in a relationship despite all odds," Taylor replied.

"Wow, I'd read that. I don't usually check out romance novels, but I'd be happy to read your manuscript if you trust me with it," Griffin said.

"Trust you with it? What kind of question is that? I trust you with my life," Taylor said.

Suddenly there was an awkward silence. *Wow, Taylor's really into me,* Griffin thought.

As strange as it seemed, Griffin felt like he had known Taylor from birth. Sure, they had dated for almost a year minus the summer they hardly saw each other. They had been through some ups and downs of their relationship, but this time felt different than before. This time Griffin felt a comfortable, peaceful feeling about Taylor and about them. It was odd, but very familiar. Griffin couldn't quite connect the dots. But he would eventually find the missing path.

Taylor smiled at Griffin with quiet confidence, with glassy eyes glued on Griffin.

Well there you have it, Griffin. She's the perfect girlfriend for you, Griffin thought.

"There's only one problem," Griffin said as he was thinking out loud.

"What did you say?" she asked.

"I didn't say anything," Griffin replied.

"Oh, yes you most definitely did," Taylor said.

"Okay, I'll go ahead and say it," Griffin replied.

Taylor's eyes look puzzled as she waited for Griffin's answer.

"It pains me to know I still have three more months of touring left before I can get home. I don't know how we're going to continue our relationship while I'm on the road," he confessed.

"I could come with you," Taylor said.

"As much as I love you, Taylor, I'm not sure if that would work," Griffin replied. "You know Turnbull's strict policy of no girlfriends or partying while on tour."

Those words pained Griffin to have to tell Taylor.

"What do you mean, you don't know if it would work out? We could make it work. Turnbull doesn't have to know. And, yes, I really, really love you too. I want to spend my life with you," Taylor said.

"You do, huh?" Griffin asked.

"Yes, I really do. I feel like we've known each other forever," Taylor confessed.

There was silence.

Before Griffin could say another word, Taylor reached across the table toward him and pressed her soft, voluptuous red lips against his. Griffin felt an incredible feeling come over him when her lips met his. She gave him a long, passionate kiss. It's a wonder they could kiss as long as they did in that awkward position with their heads stretched out across the table.

Silence returned as Griffin and Taylor sat upright in their chairs.

"Did you like that?" Taylor asked.

"Are you kidding me? Of course," Griffin replied.

"Would you like another?" she asked.

"You bet I would," he answered.

Their passionate kissing and touching continued until the waiter brought them their food. Taylor and Griffin were in their own private world. They didn't care if anyone saw their passionate, romantic gestures. They forgot the time and tuned out everyone else around them. Griffin and Taylor had spent the entire afternoon in the café talking, flirting, kissing, and sharing dreams.

Griffin and Taylor spent the rest of the day window shopping and leisurely walking in downtown Laramie since the weather was unusually warm for a January day. They took an Uber back to the hotel and ended up making sweet, passionate love all night until the morning hours.

Even though Taylor was ready to spend the rest of her life with Griffin, one burning question still lingered on her mind that needed to be answered but was tabled due to their passionate distractions. It was a question she wouldn't let Griffin forget.

***

Writing this chapter, I realized, I had never been more comfortable with a woman than I was with Taylor. I felt like I had known her forever. I completely trusted her, and all I wanted to do was spend the rest of my life with Taylor.

CHAPTER THIRTY-NINE
WHAT'S WRONG WITH THIS PICTURE?

The very next morning after making love to Taylor, Griffin told her he needed some time alone to sort things out. He let her know he needed to leave her for most of the day by herself while he spent time by himself at the library. Griffin's words deeply hurt Taylor's feelings because she thought they were breaking up. Griffin reassured her he loved her deeply and wasn't going anywhere. But how could he assure her of that? How could Griffin make such an outlandish promise to Taylor without seeing and knowing the big picture?

Something was wrong. He felt like he had lived this scenario in the same town before. Griffin had to find out what was going on and why it was happening to him. He spent Monday morning and all afternoon inside the quiet solitude of the Laramie Library racking his brain, searching for clues and answers to his déjà vu experiences.

A voice in his head interrupted him.

Read your book, Griffin; the answers are in your book.

Griffin thought it was strange for him to read his own book. In fact, he knew his own book from cover-to-cover. He was the one who wrote it.

But he leaned back, legs fully stretched on the library easy chair and read the words he had written over a year ago. He read, but still found no clues or answers. Griffin read for three more hours—still no clues.

And then Griffin reached chapter thirty-seven. As he read those words, they suddenly became bone-chillingly real. Griffin heard his own words speak to him loud and clear.

"A revelation. How could this be? That's impossible," Griffin said to himself.

But there it was so plain to see. His story was so obvious. It appeared he was living out every word he had written. His book was like prophesy.

In his book, Griffin had visited Laramie, Wyoming and had a tour assistant named Elsie. Griffin had even stayed at the Hilton Hotel.

Someone stop me before I creep out, Griffin thought.

Taylor was the girl Griffin had met earlier in his book

"So, if Taylor, and I fell in love in my book, is it possible that the rest of what I wrote will could come true?" Griffin asked himself.

Don't be ridiculous, Griffin. It's only fiction, the voice in his head said.

But everything Griffin had written a year ago in his book had come true up to this moment.

"That means that Taylor…"

The thought of the horrid picture running through his mind brought deep chills to his body as he leapt out of the chair and frantically paced the floor.

What am I going to do? How could I be so foolish? How could I be so stupid?

And yet it was happening before his very eyes. The story in his book was unfolding and Griffin was living out every second, every minute, and every hour. It was real.

How could that be? I am no prophet, no magician, and I'm certainly no god, Griffin thought.

"I am an author, for God's sake," Griffin said to himself.

"Let me get this straight—I wrote a tragic scene in the final chapter of my book. Is it possible this could actually happen in real life?"

"And if I were to re-write it at this very moment, could it become a happily-ever-after ending in real life?" Griffin continued.

Griffin had to let Taylor know immediately. Her life was at stake. Their love, their friendship, and all the happiness they shared together could tragically come to an end. Taylor had to know the truth. But would she believe him?

***

This chapter made me realize the clock was ticking and that time would run out soon for Taylor. I had to stop the final chapter tragic scene from happening.

CHAPTER FORTY
WOULD SHE BELIEVE ME?

Griffin wasted no time. He called an Uber and headed straight to the hotel. He paid the driver, walked through the front door of the hotel, and took the elevator to the second floor. Griffin stopped at the hotel door and knocked.

"Taylor, it's me," Griffin said loudly.

No answer.

Griffin knocked again. The door opened, but only revealing a tiny space. The chain lock on the door was attached. Two soft, voluptuous red lips moved to fill the tiny space in the door.

"What's the password?" Taylor asked.

"Griffin loves Taylor," Griffin replied.

"No, but close," Taylor said.

"Taylor loves Griffin," Griffin answered.

"Closer," Taylor said.

"What could it possibly be?" Griffin asked.

"I'll give you a hint. It has to do with what happened this morning," Taylor said.

"I give up," Griffin replied.

"Taylor loves and misses Griffin," she said so seriously.

"Okay, Taylor loves and misses Griffin," he said.

"Perfect, you may enter," she replied.

Taylor removed the chain on the door and opened it wide so Griffin could see her. She smiled and winked at him seductively.

"Griffin loves and misses Taylor. That's what the password should have been," Griffin said tenderly.

"Aww, I've missed you soooo much, Griffin," she replied.

All at once, Taylor wrapped her soft and gentle arms around Griffin and pulled his body tightly against hers. Their lips pressed firmly against each other's, and they passionately kissed as they moved together in sync toward the brown leather couch in the room. Suddenly, Griffin pulled away and stood up abruptly. Taylor looked him straight in the eyes with a concerned look.

"What's the matter, Griffin?"

Silence seized the moment for a few seconds. Griffin couldn't hide the worried look on his face.

"Taylor, we need to talk," Griffin said.

"Talk about what? You're not breaking up with me, are you?" Taylor asked.

"No, absolutely not. You mean more to me than anything—more than my book and my tour," Griffin replied.

"When did you realize that?" Taylor asked.

"The day you surprised me at the bookstore here in Laramie. I began to realize how self-centered and selfish I had been all my life. It's a wonder I had any friends. Before you, I only thought of myself and of becoming a famous book author, and that ruled my life. But, none of it matters anymore," Griffin confessed.

"Really?" she asked.

"Yes, I don't need fame or money in my life. I need you," he confessed.

"Seriously? "Taylor asked.

"Yes, I mean it. I need you, Taylor. I'd give up everything just to have you with me," Griffin said.

"Aww, Griffin, that's the sweetest thing anyone's every said to me," Taylor said.

She reached over with her arms and wrapped them tightly around Griffin like she'd never let go.

Then silence returned for a moment.

"I rushed over here to tell you something urgent. Your life is in danger, Taylor. I came here to warn you," Griffin said.

"Seriously?" she asked.

"Serious as a massive heart attack," he replied.

Taylor burst out in laughter.

Griffin sat in silence allowing her to chew on the words of warning he had just spoken.

"Let me understand this, Griffin. You're saying my life is in danger like the story of when Chicken Little warned all the other animals the sky was falling. Is this a sick joke?" Taylor asked.

Griffin firmly placed his hands on her arms to get her full attention. He looked her straight in the eyes.

"No, Taylor, it's not like that. This is for real—your life is truly in danger," Griffin warned.

Taylor moved a few inches away from where his body was seated.

"Griffin, now you're scaring me," Taylor said.

He moved his body closer to hers. And wrapped his arms around her. She was shaking.

"Stop telling me crazy things to frighten me," Taylor said.

"I came back here to warn you, not scare you," Griffin replied.

"But you're scaring me, Griffin."

"I'm sorry, Taylor," Griffin said tenderly as he held her body closer.

"What proof do you have that my life is in danger?" Taylor asked.

"I can explain, if you'll give me five minutes," Griffin said.

"Okay, tell me," Taylor said.

Griffin continued to hold her and look her straight in the eyes. Silence came, like the kind that comes before a storm.

"When I got to this town last Thursday before my book signing event, things were starting to feel strangely familiar. It was as if I had lived in Laramie before. I felt like I had known everyone in this town before, including Elsie and the bookstore owners," Griffin explained.

"I think we've all had those déjà vu feelings sometime in our lives, Griffin," Taylor said.

"No, but that's not what I'm talking about," Griffin replied.

"Well, what do you exactly mean?" Taylor asked.

"I mean I'm not dreaming, not hallucinating, and I'm not dead. But I know that I've been here in Laramie before. Yet, I've never set

196

foot in this town. I never even knew about Laramie until my manager put it on the map," Griffin said.

"Okay, so what's so strange about that?" Taylor asked.

"The way you surprised me after the book signing on Saturday and our relationship being reignited happened exactly the way I had written it over a year ago," Griffin replied.

"It's surely got to be a coincidence," Taylor replied.

"No, I don't think so," Griffin said.

The silence filled the space between their words.

"Okay, I'll try to explain. I started questioning myself as to why I was here in Laramie and why it all felt so familiar. I realized something was wrong with the picture. I had to find out why. That's why I asked you this morning to give me some time to sort out these strange but familiar feelings. It's like a gut instinct that I can't explain. I spent almost all day racking my brain, trying to solve the mystery. That is when it happened," Griffin said.

"What happened, Griffin?" Taylor asked.

"I heard a voice that told me to read my very own book—the answers to the mystery were found there," Griffin said.

"Now you're really creeping me out—you're hearing voices," Taylor replied.

Taylor rose from the couch and paced the floor.

"So, you think I'm crazy?" Griffin asked.

"No, I didn't say that. I said that you are hearing voices in your head, and it is scaring me," Taylor said.

"Voice, I heard one voice," Griffin said.

"Okay, go on," Taylor replied.

"I thought it was crazy to read my own book—words I knew from cover-to-cover, but I started reading and hours later, I still had no clues or answers. I continued to read. Still no answers. I put the book down to take a break. I came back and read until I got to chapter thirty-seven. That's when everything changed. It was like a major revelation," Griffin said.

"What was so revealing about chapter thirty-seven?" Taylor asked.

"I discovered that everything I had written up until now had come true. I have lived every word. It was like prophesy," Griffin said.

"I'm not sure I'm following you," Taylor replied.

"What I'm saying is that the words in chapter thirty-seven spoke to me loud and clear. It was like a revelation. They were bone-chilling real. I told myself that it was impossible. But it was so obvious. The names of the places and people were the same in my book, and I have been living out every word I wrote," Griffin said.

"That's not possible, Griffin," Taylor replied.

"That's what I thought, too. But it turns out, everything written in my book is accurate to a T, including Laramie, Wyoming where you surprised me on Saturday after my book signing. Even the hotel we are staying in now is the same hotel named in the book," Griffin said.

"That's all coincidence, Griffin. There's no proof."

"Well how do you explain that every single word I wrote has become true up until now?" Griffin asked.

The silence divided their words and conversation. Taylor was too busy thinking and couldn't answer Griffin's question.

"And I'm in the book in Laramie?" Taylor asked.

"Yes, your name is Taylor in chapter nine. That was before I met you," Griffin answered.

"Come on, Griffin, you can't possibly believe I am the same Taylor as in your book," Taylor said.

"Yes, I'm afraid so. You're the Taylor I fell in love shortly after chapter nine and the same Taylor I am falling in love with all over again here in Laramie," Griffin answered.

"Wow, this is too much to believe. You're really scaring me, Griffin," Taylor said.

Taylor's feet quickly paced the floor as she shook her head in disbelief.

"So, if I'm the Taylor in your story, then what happens to us?" Taylor asked.

Griffin's lips suddenly froze. He couldn't speak.

"What happens? Taylor asked.

Silence.

"You don't want to know," Griffin replied.

"Why not, Griffin? Does something happen to you or to me?" Taylor asked.

Griffin's lips were sealed. He was scared to tell her the truth. It would terrify her too much.

"Tell me, Griffin. Tell me the truth," Taylor raised her voice in hysteria.

Griffin stood in complete silence without speaking a word.

"If you can't tell me the truth, then we have nothing more to say to each other," Taylor said. "Tonight, you can sleep on the couch and I will sleep on the bed."

Taylor turned her back to Griffin. Her body became cold and frozen like a statue. She didn't kiss or touch him. Taylor was petrified. Griffin knew she meant business. This was a terrible way to end the night with someone you love.

CHAPTER FORTY-ONE
DO OR DIE

Griffin was panic-stricken. Was he crazy? Was he reading way too much into the words he wrote? Griffin had to do something fast. Taylor was the love of his life. He couldn't stand to lose her and to lose her in such a tragic way. Taylor had changed his life in a powerful and positive way. He was no longer self-centered and selfish. All he thought about was Taylor's well-being and pleasing her in every way possible. If Griffin called Mr. Turnbull and told him, would he look like a fool? At this point, he didn't give a rat's ass what Arnold Turnbull thought. Taylor meant everything to him. Griffin was willing to give it all up so he could save her life. Griffin and Taylor were meant to be together for eternity.

***

Enough was enough. It was time to stop hiding behind my character, Griffin, in the book. Sure, it was difficult and personal to write about myself in first person, but now was the time to let go of Griffin. I had to face this critical moment in my life by stepping out all by myself as Carlton Tucker. The only logical solution to save Taylor was to rewrite the last chapter of my book. I had to change the words before they destroyed her. If I rewrote the ending, would Mr. Turnbull approve it? Turnbull would have to agree to a second printing and to pull all my current books from the shelves. There was only one way I could find out. I decided to call Turnbull early Tuesday morning. I chose to stay two extra days in Laramie to keep an eye on Taylor and to make sure she was safe before I left. I decided to tell Elsie I was staying those extra days. I told her I had an emergency to work out. She went along with my wishes and paid for those extra nights at the Hilton on the company credit card without getting approval from Mr. Turnbull. Also, Elsie rescheduled my flight to Greeley, Colorado for Thursday afternoon.

Tuesday morning arrived and I was ready to call Mr. Turnbull. Taylor and I had spent a miserably chilly night all because I tried to warn her about her life being in danger. I had memorized what I would say to hopefully convince Turnbull that Taylor's life was in peril and that he needed to make some changes. It was eight thirty a.m., but in New York it was eleven thirty.

Tuesday morning was probably a good time to catch him, so I took the plunge and called.

"Sheldon House Publishers, may I help you?" the receptionist said.

"Mr. Turnbull, please," I said.

"May I ask who's calling?" the receptionist asked.

"This is Carlton Tucker."

I paced the floor in circles and tugged at my hair while I waited for Turnbull to answer. Suddenly, I heard that familiar deep commanding voice.

"Carlton, how are you?" Turnbull asked.

"Not so good," I replied.

"How was your flight to Greeley this morning?" Turnbull asked.

"I'm still in Laramie," I said.

"I thought you had a flight to Greeley at five after seven," Turnbull replied.

"That's what I was calling about, Sir. I had an emergency in the past few days and needed to take care of it today. Elsie booked a new flight for me on Thursday afternoon. I'm staying two extra days in Laramie, if that is alright with you," I said.

"What kind of emergency are we talking about, Carlton?" Turnbull asked.

Turnbull's voice sounded piping angry. He was curt with me and seemed to have little, if any patience left.

"It's a long story, but if you've got a few minutes I'll tell you," I replied.

"Okay, shoot," Turnbull said.

"Mr. Turnbull, I need your permission to re-write the last chapter of my book," I said.

"What the hell are you talking about Carlton? Your book is done. You signed a contract and your book has sold well over a one and half million copies so far. Why would you want to change the last chapter?" Turnbull asked.

"Because I discovered that I've been living out every word in the book I wrote over a year ago," I said.

"What are you talking about Carlton? That's impossible. This book is pure fiction, and nothing more than that," Turnbull replied.

"I made the discovery after I realized I had lived this life in Laramie before. Yet, I've never set foot in Laramie, much less Wyoming. Everyone and everything were so strangely familiar—too familiar," I said.

"Carlton, that's pure coincidence and nonsense," Turnbull replied.

"I couldn't solve the mystery of why the town and its people were so familiar until a voice in my head told me to read my very own book. So, I read it again. I couldn't find any clues or answers until I reached chapter thirty-seven. That chapter described everything and everyone in detail just as I've lived it this past week," I said.

"That's crazy talk, Carlton. Calm down. Again, it's purely coincidental," Turnbull replied.

Turnbull's voice grew louder and angrier than before.

"The strangest part was my girlfriend showed up by surprise in Laramie," I said.

"So, what, that's fiction," Turnbull said.

I paced faster around the room in circles. I'd had all I could take from Turnbull. I was ready to pull my hair out because Turnbull wouldn't budge.

"I've fallen deeply in love with her just like the way it happened in my book. But the trouble is, if what happens at the end of the book really comes true in the coming days or weeks, that would be an awful, tragic ending for Taylor," I said.

"Why does it matter? It's pure fiction," Turnbull replied.

"I'm pleading with you to change the ending of the book so that Taylor lives happily ever after."

"Boring," Mr. Turnbull replied.

"But what if the tragic ending really happens to my Taylor?" I asked.

"Trust me, it won't. You've got nothing to worry about," Turnbull answered.

"Couldn't I rewrite the ending so it doesn't end tragically? Please, Mr. Turnbull."

"No, absolutely not. The ending you wrote is brilliant. You don't need a different ending," Turnbull answered.

"But, Mr. Turnbull, I strongly believe Taylor's life is in danger and will end in the same tragic way my book ends," I said.

"Carlton, I hate to say this. But you've got some serious issues. If you truly believe what you are saying, then you need some professional help. Don't forget, Carlton, I control you. I told you before and I'm telling you again. I am the master of your destiny," Turnbull emphatically stated.

"But—"

"No, I won't allow you to change the ending. The ending was written for a reason. There's a reason for everything. If I change the ending, it will change everything about your destiny," Turnbull insisted.

Silence overtook our heated conversation as I gritted my teeth with frustration and anger. I was pissed at Mr. Turnbull. All Turnbull could think of was money and how many books he could sell. I was tired of being his servant.

"If you can't help me, I quit," I shouted.

"What do you mean by that? Turnbull asked.

"I quit," Carlton shouted louder.

"You can't quit, Carlton. You're under contract to finish your tour. Besides, I own you."

CHAPTER FORTY-TWO
THE CLOCK'S TICKING BOMB

If Mr. Turnbull couldn't help me then who could? The clock was ticking, and I was running out of time. The tragic ending of my book was almost certain to happen to Taylor at any minute. I felt helpless. Sure, I could rewrite the ending to his book, but without Mr. Turnbull's blessing, I would never be able to change Taylor's fate. Her fate was in my hands now. At least, that's what I thought.

I decided to stay in Laramie with Taylor for the time being. There'd be no more touring, no more book signings, and no more playing Mr. Nice Guy. I was thoroughly disgusted with Mr. Turnbull. In our heated conversation on the phone, he had revealed to me the mean, spiteful, judgmental, and despicable person he really was. Turnbull had become my number one enemy. And Turnbull didn't own me. I decided to get Turnbull's attention and force his hand until he approved the new ending for my book

"Let him badmouth me, cut me off, and try to destroy me, but Taylor is my whole life now, and her life is hanging by just one thread—the ending of my book," I said to myself.

"Damn you, Mr. Turnbull. I personally hold you responsible if anything should happen to her," I shouted out loud.

CHAPTER FORTY-THREE
THAT SHOULD DO IT

Mr. Turnbull slammed the phone down with all his strength. His heated conversation with Carlton was too much for him. He shoved a stack of files and a large glass vase onto the floor. The tile was covered in shattered glass with papers scattered everywhere. Turnbull called his receptionist as he paced the floor beside his desk.

"Kelsey, hold my calls. I'll be busy for a while," Mr. Turnbull said.

"Yes, sir," she replied.

Turnbull reached for his laptop on the desk and sat in his chair. His fingers typed furiously. His eyes were glued attentively to the screen.

"That little twerp still doesn't get it. He thinks he can tell me what to do. If only Carlton knew I've been writing his whole life story all this time. I control everything about him," Turnbull said.

Turnbull continued to type. He was a like a hot, steaming boiler ready to blow.

"That loser thinks he's going to quit the tour, give up on being an author, and spend the rest of his life with that girl in Laramie. Well, I'll show him who's in control. He'll be sorry he ever double-crossed me," Turnbull continued. He continued to type at a frantic pace.

"I created him, and I own him. By God, he'll do what I say," Turnbull shouted out loud.

Finally, Turnbull stopped typing and leaned back in his chair with his arms folded and stretched behind him. A sweet smile of revenge appeared on his face. Suddenly, loud, dark, evil laughter came out of his vocal cords and mouth. His laughter pierced the walls and floors of the adjoining offices. Turnbull sounded like the devil who had just conquered the world.

"That should do it."

CHAPTER FORTY-FOUR
THE FINAL CHAPTER

Late Wednesday morning, my phone rang but I didn't answer. I left Taylor at the hotel room while I had a farewell business meeting with Elsie at the Crawdaddy Bar and Grill on East Iverson Street. I sat at the café table and in the middle of the meeting my phone rang again. I jumped up from the table and rushed out of the restaurant to take the call. A familiar voice frantically screamed on the other end.

"Help, help me, Carlton, don't let me die!" the panicked voice cried.

I was stunned. Before I could say a word, another voice came on the phone.

"Your girlfriend gets a bullet in her head if you don't bring me the money," the loud rough male voice demanded.

I stuttered and froze in a state of shock. Suddenly my adrenaline kicked in.

"You better not do anything to my girlfriend," I yelled.

"You've got until four p.m. Get me the money, now," the male voice commanded.

"What money?" I asked.

"The money you made from selling your book," the man shouted.

"I haven't seen any money yet," I replied.

"Bullshit," the man roared. "A hundred grand or your girlfriend's brains will be splattered all over these yellow-painted walls,"

I wondered how the man holding my girlfriend hostage knew I got a $100,000 advance.

"Are you there, asshole?" the man hollered.

"Yes, but don't hurt my girlfriend," I replied.

I froze in a panicked state. My arms and legs shook uncontrollably. I couldn't breathe.

"The bank's open now. Bring me that money and your girlfriend lives," the man demanded.

"I'm on my way," I replied nervously.

"Don't think about calling the cops, FBI, swat team, or any kind of cop. If you do, your Taylor dies," the voice warned.

The phone went dead. And dead is what Taylor would be after four p.m. if I didn't deliver the money. I only had $75K left in the bank after being robbed of $9K, spending money on the party, my bike and other purchases. $75K would have to do. I would have to convince the man holding Taylor at gunpoint to accept less money. I would have to lay a sad story on the man and maybe, he might show me mercy. It was a huge risk. What if Taylor didn't make it? I would live with the guilt and pain for the rest of my life. I loved Taylor with all my heart. It would destroy me if I lost her.

I returned to the table where Elsie and I were meeting and excused myself.

"Sorry, but I've got to go take care of something immediately," I said.

"Are you okay, Carlton?" Elsie asked.

"Yes," I answered.

I hurried out of the café and rushed to the bank. Fortunately, my bank, Bender Bank was located a block away from the restaurant. I sprinted into the bank, showed my ID and pleaded with the teller to withdraw all the money in my account. Fortunately for me, the bank had the money on hand and large bills. I carefully placed them into my wallet and hurried to the hotel in an Uber to deliver the money

The Uber driver dropped me off at the rear parking lot of the hotel at 12:51 p.m. It was good I had arrived almost three hours early. Perhaps I could surprise the kidnapper and catch him off guard. I stood behind a tall U-Haul truck staring at the second-story window of the room where the abductor held Taylor captive. I pondered about what my plan might be. Whatever I decided, it would be dangerous and very risky facing the kidnapper. If I tried to foil the abductor, Taylor and I could be killed.

I finally decided what to do. But if I had to die, I would take a bullet for Taylor so she might live. I noticed that the hotel rooms closest to the outside had balconies. I climbed up onto the first-floor balcony and looked around to see if anyone was watching. Luckily, the drapes were drawn shut to the sliding glass door on the metal deck where I stood. Then I stood on the railing of the balcony and reached with all my might, trying to grab hold of the second balcony rails. Somehow, I managed to grab the railing with both hands and pulled my body up to the second-level deck. I showed unbelievable strength as my adrenaline pumped through my veins. I stood on the second-story deck. My eyes peered through the glass door as I hid behind the covered part of the door where the drapes were drawn.

I peered through the glass and caught a glimpse of the assailant from behind. He had short dark hair with a medium height and build. The kidnapper stood facing the front door, holding Taylor tightly in his arm and pointing an automatic gun to the back of her head. I quietly slid the glass door open wide enough for me to step inside and sneaked through the door without the kidnapper noticing me.

Without warning, I rushed the captor with all my might, striking him in the lower legs and ankles with my body, much like a football player is tackled in a professional game. The kidnapper fell forward to the floor as Taylor escaped the clutch of his hands and ran for her life. She managed to dial 911 on her phone but was too panic-stricken to tell them anything. She was speechless. The 911 dispatchers remained on the line and listened to the ongoing fight between the kidnapper and me. The dispatchers were attempting to find the location of the hotel.

My body was on top of the abductor as we wrestled for the gun. The gun went off in our struggle, and a stray bullet struck the wall. After minutes of fighting over control of the gun, the kidnapper rolled on top of me and shoved both of his hands around my neck. I choked and gasped for air as the attacker tightened his death grip around my esophagus. My face turned blue from lack of oxygen. Taylor, aware I was helpless and couldn't fight for myself, grabbed a large, heavy glass vase and smashed it over the back of the kidnapper's head. The abductor fell limp for a moment as I broke free. I rushed for the gun with my hands as the kidnapper stood up. The captor charged me at the same time I picked up the loaded gun from the floor. Seconds before the kidnapper tackled me; the gun went off in my hands and struck the abductor in the chest. He fell to the floor and was profusely bleeding.

I stood frozen with the gun still in my hand and pointed at the kidnapper. Taylor totally froze where she was standing in her tracks, totally panic-stricken as the police and EMT paramedics kicked the front door open. The police surrounded me and the wounded kidnapper on the floor.

"Freeze, drop your gun," an officer shouted.

The gun fell to the floor, and the police grabbed my arm and moved me to the couch nearby. The paramedics surrounded the kidnapper's body and gave him IVs while trying to stop the bleeding. The abductor was still conscious as the paramedics laid him on a stretcher and carried him to the EMT vehicle.

After questioning Taylor and me for over an hour, the police decided to let us both go. The officers could clearly see Taylor and I were not murderers. We were trying to defend ourselves from the abductor and save both of our lives. Taylor explained how the kidnapper had hidden outside in the hallway and waited for her to answer the knock at the door. She assumed it was me knocking and opened it. A man forced his way into the hotel room and covered Taylor's mouth so she couldn't scream. He had roughed Taylor up, choking her neck, strong holding her body into a strangled position, and threatened to blow her brains out. According to Taylor, she tried to fight the abductor and screamed for help but felt powerless to do much else with an automatic weapon shoved against her skull. The abductor found Taylor's phone and dialed my number demanding ransom money for Taylor's release.

I explained how I had surprised the kidnapper by entering the glass balcony door and forcefully tackling the captor. I told the officers how the kidnapper and I wrestled on the floor and how the gun accidentally fired, injuring the captor. While being interviewed by the officers, Taylor and I learned the would-be kidnapper had died on the way to the ER. Charges were never filed against me for accidentally shooting the man. Taylor was forever grateful to me for saving her life and felt beholden to me, her "hero."

After Taylor's kidnapping and close call of death, she and I grew even closer. We both realized we couldn't live without each other. We knew how much we needed one another and how the love we shared was undeniable and uncontainable. So, I found the opportune time to ask Taylor to be my wife in marriage by surprising her at a romantic dinner in Laramie's finest restaurant with an extraordinary, exquisite ring I had bought with some of the money the kidnapper never got.

Taylor and I married in a small chapel ceremony two days later. After our wedding, I continued my book tour for Sheldon House Publishers with Taylor by my side. Mr. Turnbull couldn't keep Taylor from touring with me since we were husband and wife. I was pleasantly surprised Mr. Turnbull finally listened to me as far as making changes to the final chapter. As a result, Turnbull had the best book sales ever after reluctantly changing the final chapter from a tragedy to a happy, romantic ending. What Turnbull thought was a boring ending turned out to be a big hit with readers worldwide. The newly changed *A Novel Life* was enormously successful and it remained on top of the *New York Times* Bestsellers list for weeks, selling a record number of copies.

But something had to give. I could no longer be a servant and character in Turnbull's book. I could no longer be controlled by Turnbull. I had all I could take.

Soon I *will* begin writing the sequel to my first book. But this time I *will* be the only author, and no one will be the master of my destiny.

-   The End

About the Author

Ever since his mother signed him up for piano lessons at age five, Thornton Cline has been writing non-stop. With over 1,000 published songs, 150 recorded songs, 32 traditionally published adult, children's and YA books published, Thornton Cline has been nominated multiple times for Grammy and Dove Awards. In 2017, Cline won a first-place Maxy Literary Award for "Best Children's Young Adult Book". Thornton Cline's books have appeared at the top of the Amazon bestselling charts. Cline has been honored with "Songwriter of the Year" twice-in-a row and has received a platinum award for certified sales of over one million units in Europe.

Cline continues to mentor, speak, teach, and inspire aspiring authors and songwriters around the world. He resides in Hendersonville, Tennessee with his wife, Audrey and two cats, Kiki and Gracie. You can follow all the latest updates on his books and songs at his website, ThorntonCline.com; Thornton Douglas Cline on Facebook, @ClineThornton on Twitter, and @ThorntonCline on Instragram. *A Novel Life* is Thornton Cline's debut book with SYP Publishing.